ARENA SL

Ian Smith

ARENA SLAVE – BOOK 2

FETISH WORLD BOOKS

A FETISH WORLD BOOKS PAPERBACK

ISBN: 978 1 78695 620 0

FETISH WORLD BOOKS
is an imprint of
Fiction4All

This Edition Published 2021
Fiction4All

CHAPTER ONE

David Harrington, Raffle Winner

I had never won a prize in my life. And here I was standing before a group of naked girls hanging from a horizontal beam. They would be whipped until, one by one, they lost their grip in their anguish and fell off. (A soft landing mat had been thoughtfully placed under each team: after all, nobody wanted to damage the property of either team's owner!) The raffle prizes, three to supporters of each team, were the opportunity to be the ones doing the whipping; and, as winner of the first prize for A.C. Tigresses supporters, I would do the whipping of their lovely new girl, Nicky Nipples.

So, as one of the three winners, I stood, whip in hand, staring up at the three naked girls hanging precariously from their beam, each of whom was looking down at me and my two companions with much less enthusiasm. Close up, their beauty was intoxicating and the organisers were letting the tension build, as well as allowing the girls' arms to get really tired, before they started, so I had time to study the girls at my leisure. An audience of over 300 people, 95% of them men, were also drinking in the loveliness of both teams of girls, but I was right up close.

Slightly to my left was Slave Katie Cunt. She was just eighteen; ah, sweet eighteen and cute as a kitten. Her fine, light brown hair was brushed back from her forehead, just a few strands escaping to stick to her sweating brow and her hair was just about long enough to tie back. More sweat, caused by her exertions so far this afternoon and the hot spotlights illuminating the arena in which we stood, ran from her hairless armpits and down her flanks. With her arms up, her already slender figure looked even more boyish, only the slightest bumps of her breasts evident, the nipples decorated by the two gleaming silver rings which had already been used to cause her considerable anguish, the poor thing.

My eyes lowered a little. Her stomach was always flat, but in her hanging position looked even thinner, her tiny waist as thin as could be. Her crotch was totally devoid of hair, which made her look even younger and more vulnerable. She was bald because her team had been on a losing streak of late and one girl from each losing team always has her crotch publicly shaven after a defeat. It had been Katie's turn, I recalled from today's programme, two weeks ago and there were no real signs yet that her bush was beginning to grow back.

My eyes finished their sweep, admiring the trim yet nicely, ever so slightly muscled legs of the trained gymnast she had been before her enslavement. Her cute toes dangled some eighteen inches off the floor. She was a light girl, a mere 48 kilos according to the match stats page and her slim arms, again from her gymnastics and other former sporting hobbies, were quite strong, but they would already be aching from supporting her weight for some five minutes now. Well, she would soon be aching a good deal more, all over.

I switched my gaze to the girl on the right, Slave Gemma Jism. She was short, around the same height as Katie, but rather more stockily built. No way were her boobs going to disappear like Katie's with her arms stretched up! Her jet-black hair was a little longer than Katie's and a little more voluminous, but seemed to stay nicely in place, caressing her bare shoulders when she stood normally. With darker hair, you could see from this distance just the faintest dots of armpit hair and soft, almost downy hair on her upraised arms; and, beneath the firm young breasts and a stomach just slightly more curved than Katie's, her crotch was showing short, dark stubble as her pubic hair began to grow back from a similar public shaving to Katie's, a couple of weeks previously. That stubble must itch a bit and to have people able to see it grow week by week - but then, such a lack of privacy was par for the course for these poor victims of our system. Gemma's short but curvy legs, like Katie's, were more or less relaxed, whilst the third hanging girl, Nicky, was keeping her legs more tightly pressed together. Katie and Gemma weren't wasting their strength that way. Neither of them liked being exposed as they were, but it was slowly becoming a fact of life for them.

On the other hand, the girl in the middle, Slave Nicky Nipples, my actual target, was a first timer in lots of ways. Like just about every spectator in today's audience, I'd read the programme notes about her with avid anticipation. She was quite a find: just eighteen, not a virgin but still fairly innocent and a fit, sporting girl: a recent World Karate medallist, no less. What was even better and had whetted the appetite of everyone in the audience, was that she had never been whipped. They had managed to enslave her with threats and demonstrations of what happened to others who resisted. Even now, after six events in today's match, she had not felt the kiss of the lash. She'd felt the pain of weights hung from her brand new nipple and labia rings, but that was it. She should have felt the whip by now, but in her whipping match she had avoided getting hit even once by using her karate to disable her opponent in the first few seconds. Very smart, but now her luck had run out: she could not avoid the whip any longer and she knew it. She stared down at me, her wide blue eyes like those of a rabbit staring hypnotised into the lights of an oncoming truck. Fear vied with determination on her pretty face.

I smiled at her and let my gaze wander down her body. She had very good boobs, firm and shapely, the small nipples bedecked with the new silver rings she would already doubtless have come to hate. Her arms were superbly toned, just the right side of being muscular, but I suspected with plenty of power in them from her karate training. She gripped the overhead bar with conviction and, although the heaviest of the three Thornton girls at around 60 kilos, her arms were not yet suffering with taking the weight of her body - though they inevitably would in time. My eyes inched leisurely down to the trim stomach, its taut muscles impressive, and then I came to the triangle of dark red curly pubic hair. Earlier I had watched this lovely young girl miserably expose herself, stripping stark naked in front of a large crowd of onlookers for the first time in her previously fairly sheltered life. Now, in her mortification, her thighs were pressed closely together, so that the small silver rings, already barely visible beneath the lush pubic hair, were now pushing into the firm flesh of those thighs and her shapely legs with their silky skin were together at both knees and ankles. She would be better advised to relax, to save all her lactic acid and energy for her arms, but of course that was easy for me to say.

My eyes returned to her face. She knew that I'd been looking at her body and her cheeks blushed red. Of course, several hundred men had been admiring her bare charms for the last hour or two, but up close it was even more humiliating. However, her eyes flicked continually to the whip in my hand. I put it behind my back and her eyes returned to my face. I tried to read her expression: there was suffering and misery there and also a degree of bewilderment: for all that she had seen a match last week, I don't think she could quite believe the things she had been forced into so far today. But also her features showed a growing determination, a desperate but substantial courage. As she looked at me, she knew her body was on display and she pressed her thighs firmly together, for all that it didn't help much; but she could do nothing about her breasts. And then I brought the whip in sight again and her eyes went to that once more; but then they left the whip and settled on my face once more. It was a sort of acquiescence: I know you are going to whip me, said those blue eyes, and I am afraid; but I accept that it is going to happen and I will endure it as best I can and for as long as I can. As is so often the case with slave girls, there was no hatred or resentment there: intimidation and fear wash those emotions away. I readied the whip and saw her tense, her breath catching in her throat, her muscles locked, her heart no doubt pounding.

The buzzer went to signal us to begin.

I swung the whip almost leisurely. It made contact with her hip and the tip swung round and bit into her bottom. "Ow!" she cried and that supple young body jerked with the shock of it. I always target the bottom first: although there are many varied and delightful ways to torment a female slave, the most basic and fundamental is to beat her bottom. A slave girl must learn that the purpose of her bottom is to receive pain and that her bared ass is always a potential receptacle of that pain. I swung the whip again, the other side this time and again it wrapped around her hip and the end bit into her nether cheeks. It was a light, thin whip, but with a knot close to the tip and it would be the knot that caused most of the effect. I swung again and again, alternating sides, eliciting a gasp of anguish each time. From nearby came a cacophony of squeals from all six girls as their tormentors found their targets, but my focus was solely on this lovely creature before me. After six strokes around each hip, I shifted my aim a little higher, letting her bare back get its first taste of the whip. She shuddered and bit her lip, but if anything her gasps were growing quieter, although she was wincing very nicely. One girl on each team had fallen already. I noticed that Katie was still up, writhing but staring at Nicky, as if she was taking a lead from this virgin to the whip.

I gave Nicky's back a good roasting, then shortened my grip for extra control and flicked at her stomach. Four, five times the knot left angry red marks on the tensed, muscular belly. Time to go up a bit. The knot landed squarely on her ringed nipple (I was pleased with my shooting on that one!) and she yelped, but still her fingers clutched that bar. I was impressed. I went for the other nipple, but this wasn't the easiest of whips to control and I missed, the knot digging into her tender breast flesh instead (with plenty of effect), but my second try hit the mark. I then went back and hit her other breast as if that had always been my intention. She was yelping now with each shot and I could see tears of both shock and pain rolling down her cheeks, but still she held on. Another Tigress girl had gone, but the team I supported could still yet win the day. I gave Nicky another dig on each of her stretched boobies, then paused, lengthening my grip and measuring my next shot. In her anguish, her legs had relaxed, drifting apart as she found more pressing things than her lack of modesty to contend with and that gave me a chance. I sent the whip into her thigh and it wrapped round the back and came through the middle into the front, the tip burying itself into her inner thigh. Perfect! Nicky shrieked and danced in mid-air, but still somehow she hung on. As the whip fell away, a bright red line appeared on her leg. Her limbs were flailing about too much for me to get a good shot on the other leg, so I contented myself with another couple of fierce hits on her bum, then shortened my grip again and sent the tip whizzing into those soft cherry red pubic curls of hair that she was in danger of having shorn if her team lost this match. Nicky's eyes, previously half-closed and misty with tears, opened wide and she squealed again. I think I got her right on the clitoris. I tried another similar shot, but missed a little, although the impact on her groin still very clearly hurt. Still she hung on! Let's go for her arms then, I thought. Her sensitive, hairless left armpit took a stinger; she shuddered but still clung to the bar, her knuckles white with the effort. I lined up another one, but as I did the buzzer went. I looked around: the last Tigress girl had fallen. Nicky still hung, sobbing, and nearby Slave Katie was also still up, her elfin body wracked with her sobs.

I let my whip fall to the ground with a feeling of disappointment. I had not been able to help my team avoid defeat and in one sense I had not bested the naked young beauty before me; but in another sense I had, because she now knew for the first time in her young life how it felt to be a whipped slave. And I had enjoyed myself immensely.

Life - for those in Corvalle not burdened with the yoke of slavery - was wonderful. Nicky, right now, might not agree!

CHAPTER TWO
Nicky

Ow, ow, ow, ow oww!

I hung from that bar, my arms and shoulders throbbing with the pain of taking my weight, but the pain in my body was worse.

I had just endured my first whipping. I had hung naked from a bar in front of hundreds of people and let a man whip me. It had not been from choice: there were even worse things in this terrible land if I did not comply. But oh, this had hurt!

We had won. I was still up on the bar. So, bless her, was Katie. She had been as good as her word and stuck with me, although she looked in as bad a shape as me. We had won. One more victory and I would avoid being raped by dozens upon dozens of these bastards in the audience, in addition to a vicious caning. It had been worth it. But oh, it had hurt!

The man who had whipped me was standing in front of me, admiring both his handiwork and my bare body. My nudity didn't seem so important now. I hadn't thought that a couple of hours ago when I had undressed, completely, in front of this crowd, up on a platform where everybody could see me. That had been very hard to do, as this had been hard; but I had done it, like this, to avoid the even worse fate that would have happened to me if I did not go along with these people. I knew, even now, that I had made the right decision. What they would have done to me if I had not did not bear thinking about.

Katie and I were told we could come down. My numb fingers gratefully released their grip and I collapsed in a heap. Fortunately, there was a soft landing mat beneath me. As I lay in a crumpled heap, fresh pain shot through my arms and shoulders which had taken my weight for so long. It was barbaric, the things they were doing to us. And yet, I had won. There was a pride, amidst all the humiliation of all this, to be had from that. I was one win away from safety and two events away from an end to this dreadful match. I was surviving. I was like a Christian in the Roman arena and yet I was surviving.

I struggled to my feet, aching in places I didn't know I had. Katie stood in front of me, as naked as I was. Her elfin body was covered in angry red marks and I knew my own would be the same. But she had come through it with me. Wordlessly we hugged. I felt her sweaty body tight against mine, her small breasts pressing into mine. There was even the slightest of clinks as her nipple rings clashed with mine. We were two whipped slaves together. It wasn't erotic - I've got no lesbian feelings and we were both in too much pain anyway - but it was very comforting; even a little bit inspiring.

Gemma stood hesitantly nearby. Her body also carried a fair few red marks, but she had been the first to give in. She stood uncertainly, clearly wanting to be part of the cuddle but feeling that she hadn't lasted long enough to deserve it. I let go of Katie with one arm and pulled her in. She came gratefully. We were all in this together, we had all suffered and would suffer together and Gemma had played her part in other rounds and hopefully would do again in the remaining two torments, whatever they might be.

"All right, sluts, break it up and let's be having you."

We obediently separated and stood before the steward who had spoken. I didn't hide anything of myself. I wasn't a slut but right now I felt every bit like a slave. It's funny how your mind goes when you're naked and hurting in front of several hundred men.

My hands were pulled roughly behind me. I heard a sharp click as the wristbands were clipped together. Gemma and Katie and the three Tigress girls were being similarly secured. I tugged on my bonds but they didn't give an inch. Bondage is a strange thing: it doesn't look so bad when you see it done to others but you feel so helpless and vulnerable when you're the one tied up. I really wanted to cover my chest now but instead the cuffs forced my shoulders back and made my boobs stick out.

The steward stood in front of my and grabbed one of my breasts. I winced as his fingers pressed over one of the bruises the whip had left. He pulled the breast out from my chest and with his other hand began wrapping cord around the base of it. Round and around went the cord, digging in very uncomfortably and squeezing my tit out until it bulged like and over-filled balloon. Then he repeated the process with my other udder. When he had finished, both of my boobs jutted out from my chest, the flesh red and the nipples tight. The same thing had been done to the five other girls. Six pairs of young bondaged tits stuck out from six young bodies.

We were marched to a central point in the arena and arranged in a circle, facing inwards. The crowd had a pretty good view of my whip-marked backside, but the circle was widely spread so most of them could see my front as well.

Six thick chains dangled from the ceiling. The cords constricting my chest were linked and then tied off to one of the chains. The other girls were similarly prepared. At a signal from the steward, my chain began to lift until the slack had gone. One by one, the same happened to the others. Some chains had to be lifted further where the girls were taller. All of them were now taut. I stood, my chest throbbing a little from the tightness of the cords.

Then I felt my chain rise up an inch or so.

All six girls had the same thing done to them. I raised myself up onto my toes to keep the pressure off my boobs. But how long could I stay on my toes for?

The chain rose up another inch.

I was right on my toes now and even so it was hurting badly. The cords were digging in painfully. Looking around, trying to take my mind off it, I saw the faces of my team-mates and opponents, each face showing the anguish of its owner.

The chain rose another inch. Desperately I stretched my legs, my big toes trying to keep in contact and keep my weight off my chest.

"N-no more ..."

One of the Tigress girls, Alejandra, had given way. Immediately she said that, her chain began to slacken and her feet flattened on the ground once more. I felt intensely jealous of her as her pain began to fade. I had more to take yet. I looked at Katie and Gemma. Katie was trying unsuccessfully to put on a poker face. Gemma's eyes were screwed tightly shut, but tears were still escaping them.

The chain rose another inch. Each of us now was swaying right on our outstretched toes. One more inch and our feet would leave the ground. Was it possible for a woman to hang from her breasts? Fire coursed through my bosoms. Katie and Gemma were lighter than the others: perhaps that would give them an advantage. And I? I would have to take it.

I waited for the chains to rise that last inch, but it didn't come. Instead there was a grunt to my left. One of the Tigresses, the blonde one called Helen, lurched forwards, her feet momentarily leaving the ground before her toes managed to regain their tenuous hold. I realised through the mists of my agony that a micro-second before that I had heard the sound of leather on flesh.

Whack!

Gemma gasped and swung for a moment before her toes managed to make contact once more. I realised that a steward was going around behind us, lashing each defenceless bum in turn. I would be last to get it.

The second Tigress, Anna, yelped in pain, then Katie. That left just me. I tried to steel myself.

Suddenly I felt a hot fire in my backside. The shock of it sent me swinging forwards and the pain in my bum was eclipsed by that in my chest as my feet left the ground and my entire weight made the cords dig in and seemed to squeeze my melons beyond possible endurance. Through a mist of pain my big toes somehow managed to find the deck.

One by one, the steward assaulted the rears of each girl again. I saw that it was a leather strap. As it went around the circle, ever closer to me, I watched doom approach me with miserable certainty. In due course I felt another sudden sting in my already abused behind and again I couldn't stop myself losing my footing for a few atrocious moments.

Through pounding ears, I heard a commentator say over the p.a. system, "one more round, then the chains go up again."

So another minute or so of this already appalling treatment, another lash of the leather over my already burning nates and then I would be hanging from my boobs, not for a second or two but continuously. How could I possibly bear it? I looked around the other perspiring, quietly crying girls. The two remaining Tigress girls looked frightened. They knew that if they surrendered now, their side had lost the match, with all the horrors that implied. Gemma and Katie were both trying to look brave and strong. They were relying on me. I couldn't back out now.

The Tigress girl to my right yelped as the strap swiped her bum.

Gemma squealed as her bum took its turn.

The other Tigress yelped as her friend had done.

Katie gasped bravely.

I cringed, then called out in pain as another layer of fire was added to my intolerably throbbing rear.

And then I felt a final, irresistible tug on the chain. My straining feet left the floor. Pain lanced through my chest as my full weight was taken on the cords cutting into my feminine charms.

Through mist-clouded eyes I saw Katie, doing her best to totally relax in the theory that it would be slightly less painful. Her head back, her tomboyish figure twitching in her agony, her arms by her sides, her legs limp. She was softly crying. Gemma, her bigger boobs quite misshapen, her face convulsed with her suffering, toes straining at the ends of her short but curvy legs, hopelessly trying to reach the ground. The two Tigress girls were biting their lips, trying to hold back from screaming. I closed my eyes. How long could I bear this for? Not long, surely! Why couldn't those Tigress girls just give in? I wanted, oh how I wanted, to give in and spare myself. No, no, I couldn't let Gemma and Katie down like that. I had to tough it out. Come on, Tigresses, give in, please!

As if on cue, Helen surrendered. She was lowered achingly slowly back to the ground. Anna knew that their team was now beaten whatever she did. She too gave up. Katie, Gemma and I were crying out our surrenders just moments later; but the stewards sadistically left us dangling for long seconds as they released the Tigresses before we too were lowered to earth. Oh, the relief, the relief, as the chains went slack! A steward roughly undid the cords on me and pulled them off. I screamed as the cord which had embedded itself deeply in my tender flesh was pulled away. I looked at Gemma and Katie. Each girl had a bright red mark around each of her boobs, the skin angrily red with burns from the cord. I knew I was no better. Even with the cords gone, the rope burns hurt terribly.

We fell once more into each other's arms. The score was 5-3: we could not be beaten now. Today, at least, my pubic hair would not be shaved; we would not between us be raped by well over a hundred men; and, although we would be caned, which would be yet another new nightmare experience for me, we would avoid the much more severe caning which the Tigresses were now doomed to receive.

But there was no mood of celebration: we were all hurting far too much for that. And there was yet one more event still to come.

Exhausted and battered though we were, they were already herding us towards the pony carts.

Subtly different to last week's carts, these were still three-girl carts but with two level berths at the front and a third behind the first two. Katie and Gemma were being fitted into the front two positions. They stood passively whilst they were harnessed up; I saw Katie open her mouth and watched them put a bit into it. I wondered what it would be like, to be a pony girl: I knew I was about to find out. They finished harnessing Katie and Gemma and then I was led to my berth behind them.

A thick leather band was buckled around my waist. From my right hip, another thick strap was pulled up diagonally over my back - I winced as it came down over several whip marks - and over my left shoulder. Narrowing now, it was brought down my chest - they pushed my boob out so that it would come inside it, ignoring the new pain that caused me as it moved the rope burns - and connected to the waist band. A similar strap went from my left hip over my right shoulder and down again. A thinner strap from high up the back of the thing then came round to the front, clipping each of the diagonal straps onto it and holding the whole thing firmly in place.

In order for them to connect the front straps to the waist band, I had to bend forwards. I must have looked almost ape-like and my rear end jutted out like ... I tried not to think about that. My face was level with Katie and Gemma's bums and very close to them, so close that I could see and smell the tangy perspiration on their skin from their various exertions. Katie's bottom was, like the rest of her, small and almost boyish, with occasional hints of extremely fine blonde hair; Gemma's was more rounded, totally hairless and with a superb complexion.

Almost peeping out from between Katie's and Gemma's bare bodies, I saw a short, fat, piggish man waddling towards us. He came up to Katie and a slimy flipper of a hand reached out and stroked her exposed breast. I could see her face, side on, and although the bit obscured any expression, her eyes told of her revulsion. He transferred his attention to Gemma's breasts, weighing one of them in his hand thoughtfully. I steeled myself, hating every moment of this; sure enough, a few moments later he ran his greasy finger across one of my boobs. I wanted to be sick.

"Put bells on 'em," he wheezed to the steward; "I like bells on 'em." The steward rummaged in a box and produced two tiny silver bells which he clipped to Katie's nipple rings, then two more for Gemma and finally two for me. I closed my eyes with the humiliation of it: he wanted us belled, so we were belled. The bells were quite light and their hanging from my rings was only slightly uncomfortable, but the sheer lack of any say in the matter, added to yet another reminder of why my nipples had been pierced, and being belled like a domestic cat ... it was all so hard to take that I was struggling to breathe.

Then the piggish man lumbered behind us and sat in the cart. I felt the springs sag under his considerable weight. He now had a close-up, uninterrupted view of my bum and I was bent over in the most undignified of poses. My face, if it is possible, went even redder. I closed my eyes in shame. I would now have to strain every muscle to pull this pig around the race track in front of hundreds of slavering men.

But I had to open them again as the hooter went to start the race.

The whip cracked, the tail missing me narrowly and burying itself into Gemma's bent over posterior. She shrieked and pulled with all her might.

Frightened by that whip, I did the same. My bare toes scrambled for purchase on the rough wooden floor and I pushed myself forwards, feeling the inertia of the cart holding me back through the harness. Inch by inch we began to move forwards, the silver bells attached to each of us tinkling. I could see Katie's lithe, toned young muscles rippling beneath the firm skin of her buttocks and Gemma's legs looking their shapeliest as her muscles also flexed. We were moving now and picking up pace.

Crack!

"Aaiieee!"

The whip came within inches of my ear and Katie squealed in anguish as it stung her poor defenceless bottom. Sweat was already pouring out of me and now I broke out in a fresh, cold sweat. The pig in the driving seat had deliberately whipped both girls first to frighten me and it had worked. I knew that the next time he used the whip, I would get it. It wasn't fair: I was putting in every ounce of effort I could muster and then some. So were the other two, but although not a particularly big girl, I was the heaviest of the three of us and certainly the strongest. My karate training, the exercise and discipline of both mind and body, had given me considerable physical power: now I had to use it in a way my coach Vic had surely never foreseen.

But the other team, I could see, were moving faster than us. The match was a pursuit, each cart starting half way round the track from the other and it would be the first cart to catch the other. For all her fitness and determination, I knew that we had a heavy handicap with Katie's slight stature and Gemma wasn't a lot bigger, being rounded but fairly short. Although I was no heavier than anybody in the Tigress team, thanks to my years of karate I was probably stronger than any one of them; but there were three of them pulling the other cart. Still, even if we lost this round, we had won overall.

Crack!

"Yeeowwww!"

Somehow I recognised my own voice as the whip stung my defenceless bum like half a dozen wasps all getting me at once. Oh God, it hurt! My yelp whistled past my bit and, caught unawares, a little saliva came out. Because of the bit, I couldn't close my mouth nor, with my arms secured at my sides, wipe it away. I had to just let it dribble down my cheek.

I tried, I really tried, to pull harder.

Crack!

"Aarrggggh!"

The second stroke was like a dozen wasps stinging me all at once. It was dreadful and merciless.

It's hard to explain what happened next. Basically, I just lost it. The animal inside me took over. Why not? I was naked as an animal is, harnessed like an ox, a bit in my mouth like a horse, whipped like a dog and treated like a beast of burden. The man in the seat behind me might be piggish but he was a lot more human than I right now. I lost sight of everything except the need to work, to pull that cart, to avoid the whip, to convey my rider around the track and catch the other animals pulling the other cart. It no longer mattered that I was naked, bells clinking as my unfettered tits undulated up and down. My legs were on fire with my effort, the breath whistling past the bit, my hair flying behind me. In fairness, Katie and Gemma, particularly Katie, were also pulling their hardest, but I was pulling as hard as the two of them put together. We were catching the other cart despite the odds. They increased speed as their driver whipped them, but still we closed. Demoralised, they couldn't keep up the pace. Somehow, painfully but unflinchingly, we did. Our driver cracked the whip in the air a couple of times, but didn't whip us. The Tigresses screamed as they were whipped, but it was flogging a dead horse. We caught them.

The bit in my mouth dug deeply and the reins attached to the head part of my harness pulled my head back as we were brought to a stop. My breath was burning in my chest as I gasped for air and my legs felt on fire. I wanted to collapse but the harness made it impossible and I had to stand whilst the stewards came over and began to release us. As we were freed, Katie, Gemma and I sank to the ground in total exhaustion. We were completely done in.

So were the Tigresses, but their ordeal was far from over. The two other players on their squad, who had not competed today, stepped dejectedly into the arena centre and pulled off their outfits to reveal their naked bodies to the slavering audience. One of them was already shaven. They sat down on the floor and allowed themselves to be secured into leg stocks, their legs indecently wide apart. Already queues were beginning to form for each of them as some spectators made their way down from the audience seating. Others in the audience, however, were still watching avidly as the cute blonde girl in the active Tigress team had her legs put into stirrups, giving an even more indecent display. Her blonde hair soon disappeared beneath thick white clouds of shaving foam. When the foam was scraped away with a razor, her pubic hair came away with it to reveal bare pink skin and now totally exposed sex lips, almost pouting and with the twin rings completely exposed. The girl's now hairless crotch was wiped with a towel to remove the last vestiges of foam and sundered hair and there was a small cheer from some parts of the audience as the freshly shaven victim stood up miserably.

And it got worse. I could already hear gasps and moans from the two girls on the floor as their first rapists brutally used them, but the three active girls were being put into solid-looking stocks. Three trembling young backsides jutted out towards the crowd; the stocks were arranged facing in, but in such a way that everyone in the crowd could see at least one nude backside and one face. A steward stood by each girl, holding an evil-looking cane.

Thwack!

The three canes were wielded almost simultaneously. The sound of wood biting into bare flesh sent a shudder through me. I felt myself go hot and cold as the canes struck again and again, the girls, stoic at first, soon gasping with each stroke, then moaning, sobbing and eventually almost screaming, their cries picked up by the ever-present microphones. This was unbelievably barbaric: it could not be happening, but it was. This was what I had escaped so narrowly, albeit at a considerable cost of pain and self-degradation. As I watched those poor bottoms turning purple, as welt overlaid welt, it now didn't seem quite such a huge cost to pay. Sixty strokes! Each! It was surely impossible to bear; and yet they had to bear it. I felt physically sick as I watched. I was so, so sorry for those girls; and yet I was a lot gladder that it wasn't me in those stocks. It could have been!

After what seemed like an eternity, the caning finished. The girls were released from the stocks, sobbing uncontrollably. Even now their ordeal was not over. Moving extremely gingerly, hands clutching their thrashed rears, they stumbled towards their comrades in the rape racks. Each girl howled in fresh pain as they had to sit down on their lacerated buttocks. They barely noticed as their legs were pulled wide and secured in that dreadfully vulnerable, humiliating position; and then each girl all but disappeared as the first men clambered on top of them and began to rape them.

Horrible, awful, dreadful. I had seen this last week; but now, naked and involved in a match myself, it felt so much closer to home. Suddenly I felt an arm round me: Gemma was there, trying to comfort me, realising the effect this was having on me.

"Come on," she said gently; "it's our turn in the stocks."

Her words hit me like a tidal wave. “What? But we won!”

“I know: it’s great. But we lost three rounds. For the winning team, that’s five strokes each.”

“It’s only fifteen,” put in Katie almost brightly. “That’s not bad compared to the usual. Come on, it’ll soon be over.”

Somehow, dazed and confused, I found myself being led by my two team-mates up to the stocks.

CHAPTER THREE
Narrator

Nicky was absolutely exhausted, nearly dead on her feet.

The physical exertions of the afternoon had been considerable, but the emotional ordeal had been even more draining. Nicky was not actually shy but was certainly quiet and introvert by nature, a little of a loner in some ways. Before this nightmare had started with her kidnapping, well, she hadn't been quite a virgin but she certainly hadn't done much and it was usually in at least semi-darkness. Since being kidnapped, she'd been made to take her clothes off once or twice, in front of two or three men. Nothing had prepared her for having to strip and remain naked in front of around four hundred eagerly watching pairs of eyes.

Her frame of mind, both conscious and subconscious, on being naked had varied since then. Embarrassment and humiliation were never far from the surface. At times it had bordered on catatonic: she had endured half a dozen panic attacks, sometimes bending almost double in an attempt to help her hands hide her front and acutely aware that her bottom and much of the rest of her body were still on show, wanting to crawl into a hole and pull a cover over her, until some fresh task or event brought her out of it. At other times she miserably accepted having her body on show as one of the tortures she was doomed to undergo, and sometimes this mutated into the feeling that as a slave she did not deserve clothes, that these men had the right to ogle her no matter how uncomfortable she found it. Just occasionally, when her competitive nature became fired up by one of the events, she found herself irrationally accepting that she needed to be nude for this event, so that the whip had free access to her body, or weights could be hung from her rings; or, in the final case of the pony race, simply because she was an animal, and animals do not wear clothes. It might all sound illogical in the cold calm of tranquillity, but at that time Nicky's situation was far from tranquil. Even most of these thoughts above were only pieced together gradually, painfully, in later unhappy reflection.

Nicky had also, for the first time in her life, felt the whip and many other dreadful tortures. They had hurt enormously. She had been cowed by them and yet at the same time she was proud of the courage she had been able to maintain in enduring it all.

Nevertheless, she knew, dimly at this moment but with greater clarity and certainty later, that today's nightmare experience had changed her forever. In what ways she would not know for some time, but she would never be quite the same girl again. It was a bit like losing her virginity, or gaining her black belt: only this particular change was something that didn't happen to most people, which led her to wonder so often of late. "why me?" But no answer was forthcoming.

And now she was being put into stocks to be caned. The wooden yoke, thinly padded with leather, closed over her neck and wrists, immobilising her totally. In her bent-over position, her hindquarters jutted out, presented to a substantial proportion of the crowd. But then, is there anybody in that crowd who hasn't had a good look at my bum today, she wondered. She faced Gemma and Katie, now in their own stocks and facing her like three sides of a triangle. Both girls looked tense and unhappy, but resigned.

What will the cane be like? Nicky wondered feverishly. Everybody seemed to regard it with a kind of reverence, as if it was much worse than the whip. It had certainly cut up the bottoms of the Tigress girls something terrible. Oh God, how could they be so cruel to her? With last minute desperation, Nicky tried to break out of the stocks, but it was too late. Only later did she reflect that it would have been worse for her had she been able to get out.

She sensed, although she couldn't see, the man behind her with the cane. She trembled, her tired and aching muscles spasming. Then she heard the cane whistling through the air towards her poor, already battered bottom.

Thwack!

A line of white-hot pain suddenly appeared across her bottom. Nicky yelped. It hurt, oh it hurt, oh how it hurt!

Thwack!

Another line of searing pain joined the first.

Thwack! Thwack! Thwack!

Nicky was dimly aware that the crowd was cheering. This above all was what they had come to see today: the new girl being caned. Nicky had cheated them out of part of it by her team winning the match; but she could not fully escape. She did not have that much control over her own destiny any more.

Thwack! Thwack! Thwack!

Nicky felt her bottom was ablaze. Through mist-clouded eyes she saw Katie and Gemma, their mouths open, gasping at their own pain, oblivious of hers.

Thwack! Thwack! Thwack!

How many was that? She had lost count. Surely it was fifteen!

Thwack!

Thwack!

There was a pause. Was that it? Please let it be so!

Thwack!

The last one - she somehow knew it was the last - stung the most. Then, in blissful salvation, she felt the top half of the stocks being lifted. She straightened up and pressed her fingers to her madly throbbing bottom. She could feel the hard ridges of the welts. As they turned, she saw Katie's and Gemma's bottoms, with very visible lines across them, the centre of their bums a deep red, purple in a few places. Her own bum doubtless looked much the same.

Absolutely done in, she and her two friends walked slowly, gingerly back to where Giles awaited them. They passed near to the rape racks where the five Tigress girls, three of them still sobbing convulsively, were being repeatedly raped. Nicky did not feel like a winner, but one look at these girls made her realise that it was even more terrible to be a loser.

Giles was flanked by the two unused Thornton's Fillies, both of whom looked very relieved that their team had won. They were still dressed, in their brief summer dresses; had their team lost, they would be naked in the rape racks right now. "Well done, girls," Giles said effusively. Nicky did not feel much like celebrating: every muscle in her body shook with exhaustion and a surfeit of lactic acid, the bruises all over her hurt worse and most of all her bottom pulsed mercilessly, insatiably from the caning. When he beckoned her over to him, she went and stood before him without the slightest desire to hide her charms, only a wish for her pain to ease. As he was seated, his eyes were about level with her stomach. He ran his fingers through her pubic hair. "Thought you'd lose this today," he said conversationally. Nicky did not - could not reply. She saw a glint of metal in his hands and a moment later felt the now familiar slight tug of weight. She had been chastity padlocked once more. It felt as if she were a Sunday best dinner service which, having been brought out for some guests, was now being packed away again until the next time it was needed. At least it signified that the danger of her being crowd raped was finally over, for today at least. Of course, any possibility that she might want her sexual freedom for her own ends (even though it was the last thing on her mind right now) was not to be considered. Giles handed her dress to her and turned to Katie.

Still dazed, Nicky lifted her dress over her head and slipped it on. It felt strange to be clothed once more - although it had to be borne in mind that the dress was low cut, showing plenty of cleavage, fairly tight-fitting, showing her figure and the skirt was extremely short and she had no knickers. She couldn't possibly wear any with her bottom in its current state anyway.

The moans and the groans of the Tigress girls as their unending sequence of men took them in her ears and a last glimpse of the long lines of men waiting to use them and at the banks of now emptying seats recently full of men watching her own disgrace and torment, catching her eyes, Nicky slumped off to follow the rest of her team back to Thornton's - and now her - home.

The following afternoon, the lovely Nicky was lying naked and face down on a treatment couch whilst a young man around her own age gently rubbed lotion into her bruised and welted buttocks. Trying to forget his hands on her, she was watching television, but it was no relief: she was watching "Match Of The Day", the local show which ran highlights of yesterday's matches in the league. She was watching herself, as her match was one of the two featured games. It brought back unpleasant memories, as well as the embarrassment that maybe a thousand or so people could be watching her naked form right now.

On the screen right now was the second to last event, when they had been lifted bodily off the floor by their breasts. Nicky watched her assets being distorted on the screen, wondering how anybody could find this erotic and knowing sadly that many did.

"I thought you did really well in this event," the young lad said from behind her.

"Uuhhh," Nicky moaned in shame. Tears were quietly rolling down her cheeks. As if her humiliation on the day had not been enough, to have it repeated on television and to have been ordered to watch it, dug the knife still deeper into her entrails. She wondered what Vic, her old karate coach and the man she respected above all others, would say if he saw this TV programme, saw what his star pupil had done in that arena. In revulsion, she pushed the thought away.

She felt his hand slip between her legs and instinctively pressed her thighs together, but his fingers pushed insistently deeper until they brushed the padlock. "Shame about this," he mused. "We could have had fun if you weren't locked up."

"Uuhhh," Nicky repeated. She had no desire for him at all, although she was discovering that there were many worse men in this awful city. She wondered whether, if she wasn't padlocked, he would have been able to take her. She knew that she herself would have no say in the matter. It would depend on the whim of her owner. Nicky shuddered at the thought of being owned.

The match highlights ended and the programme returned to the studio. Two smartly dressed men and a naked, pretty woman sat in easy chairs analysing the match.

The first man, the programme anchor man, spoke to the other. "Well, Alan, a surprise win for Thornton's Fillies there?"

The second man replied in a Scottish accent. "Yes, the Tigresses have done well in their last few matches. They won't be pleased with that result."

"The new girl made all the difference."

"Absolutely. She galvanised the other two. Mind, they're better than the other players in Thornton's squad. That's the strongest team Thornton could put out. The Tigresses were over-confident: some of their efforts were woeful."

The anchor man turned to the naked woman, who was clearly an ex-arena slave herself. "Would it have been particularly difficult for Nicky Nipples since it was her first time out, Sarah?"

"Terribly difficult. Her nudity would have been on her mind pretty much most of the time and she had no experience of any of the events. I thought she was fantastic."

"Of course," put in the Scot, "that's what Thornton does: he drops new girls in at the deep end. That's what their team's fans want to see."

"Do you think that Nicky can inspire the team to a few more wins?" the anchor asked the Scot.

"Maybe. Their next match isn't too difficult, but the one after that will be very tough."

"The thing is," Sarah added, "the Thornton fans are really waiting to see the poor girl lose. It's even harder to inspire team-mates when your home crowd is against you."

"Doesn't the penalties for losing help inspiration?"

"Yes they do," said the girl with a slight shudder of memory, "but that applies to both teams, remember. You need every bit of extra encouragement you can get."

"Long term, does this girl really fit in as a Thornton's Filly?"

"No. I would guess that one of the big teams will make a bid for her if she proves that this wasn't a one-off."

"Well," said the anchorman, "talking of big teams, there was a top three clash yesterday ..." and the focus shifted to another match. The terrible torment of six more unfortunate girls filled the screen.

The young man who was rubbing the lotion into Nicky's bottom finished his work. "Well, I'm off to treat little Katie. I'll be back in a few hours to give you another going over. See you later!"

As the door closed behind him, Nicky lowered her head onto the couch and closed her eyes, trying to forget her aching body and the hideous memories of yesterday and seeking the balm of sleep.

The next day, Nicky was back on duty in her maid's outfit, doing the cleaning. Despite the brevity of her skirt, she wore no knickers: her bum was still sore, although getting better. The absence of panties meant no support for her padlock and it pulled gently on her sex lips, but it had been her choice: the rubbing of the material against her healing welts would have been worse.

The domestic work itself wasn't too bad. It was monotonous, but at least she was able to be alone. After Saturday, that was a considerable relief. In any case, she had never minded working. Her great karate rival, Claire Sanderson, who was a total snob, had once archly observed that Nicky was a 'great little domestic servant.' At the time Nicky had barely controlled her temper. Now it seemed a sadly prophetic statement.

She was cleaning the lounge when Thornton breezed in and sat down with a newspaper. Nicky immediately felt nervous in his presence. This was the man who had caused her to go through the terrible events of last weekend, but she was too frightened of him to be too resentful.

"Sh-should I come back later, sir?" she asked.

He lowered the newspaper and peered over it at her. "No, that's all right; but you address me as 'Master'."

Nicky flushed. She had forgotten that. "S-sorry, Master."

He folded the newspaper away. "You're no longer leading a charmed life, girl. Mistakes have to be paid for. A smacked bottom, I think. Come here." Nicky approached, hesitantly, reluctantly. "Over my lap."

With her karate skills, Nicky could have overpowered this man fairly comfortably. But then what? Make a run for it? She had no chance of getting away, especially on the spur of the moment. Go to the local authorities? That was a joke. Just refuse? Almost as bad as running away. No, she had no choice. None at all. Mustering what little dignity she could, she came round to stand by the side of him and lowered herself across the top of his legs until her palms were on the thick carpet. She gritted her teeth, realising all too well what would come next.

As she expected, he lifted her short skirt up to expose her black and blue backside. "No knickers, eh?" Are you trying to send a message out, girl?"

She blushed furiously. "No! It was just, I was too sore there after Saturday." When I was competing for your team, she thought: can't you cut me a bit of slack?

"Hmm. Well, just remember, your pussy belongs to me. No unauthorised nookie without my permission, got it?"

"Yes ... yes, M-Master." How humiliating! And he hadn't needed to say it: the padlock kept sex out of the question.

"Now, hold still ..."

Slapp!

Even on an unblemished rear, that would have come sharp. As it was, it hurt!

Slapp!

Slapp! Slapp! Slapp!

Slapp! Slapp! Slapp! Slapp! Slapp! Slapp!

Nicky gritted her teeth and remained silent. All this for a slight slip of the tongue!

Slapp!

At last, the hand that had been holding her firmly over his lap relaxed and she was able to get back to her feet. Nicky's face was very red: the humiliation of being smacked like an errant little girl was even worse than the not inconsiderable aggravation of her still sore bruises and welts. But she wasn't out of the woods yet.

He raised an eyebrow. "Well, what do you have to say for yourself?"

She knew what she had to say. "Th-thank you for correcting me, Master," she said carefully. "I'll ...try to do better in the future."

"Hmm. You can start by going down on me."

"Master?"

He unzipped his fly and pulled out the penis that she remembered from once before. "This is what you serve, girl: men's cocks. Now give this one a good time."

Once again Nicky knew that she had no choice. It seemed that her honour was to be shredded as much as her dignity. Best to get it over with without fuss, she told herself. "D-do you have ... the key to my ..." she managed.

"I can't be bothered to go and get it. Use your mouth."

Nicky's jaw dropped open. "I - I've never done that before."

"Then you'd better be a quick learner. Get on with it."

Nicky sank to her knees in front of him. Feeling sick, she tentatively reached out her hand and her fingers touched his weapon. Fighting back nausea, she brought her face closer to it. Her tongue reached out reluctantly and touched it. There was just a light tang of salty sweat on it. It was stiffening at her touch. Closing her eyes, she opened her mouth wide and slid her lips over it.

Nicky wasn't entirely naïve: she knew what oral sex was, although she had never dreamed of actually doing it. But she wasn't sure what to do now. Guessing wildly and at the same time fighting to keep her heaving stomach under control, she ran her tongue up the underside of his manhood, then leaned back a little so he began coming out of her mouth, then forwards again to take him all in. It seemed to be working, she thought bitterly: he was growing bigger. Not for the first time, she was appalled at her meek surrender to his demands and yet she knew she had no alternative. She sucked and licked, wondering how this would end.

It ended with him suddenly going off. She felt a jet of hot come spraying the back of her throat and began to gag. At the same time she felt his hand grab her hair and hold her head in place so that she couldn't disengage. Nicky had to swallow to avoid drowning. She gulped it down, again and again and again as his cock spurted what seemed like gallons of the sticky, salty cream.

At last he was spent. The hand holding her hair let go and she was able to disengage herself. A drop of come dribbled from the side of her mouth.

"Not too bad for your first attempt. You're a quick learner. You can get back to your dusting now."

What's to learn? She thought bitterly: he sticks it in and I suck to avoid choking. And I debase myself every way possible to avoid getting into trouble with these people. But she knew how ruthless they were: getting into trouble with them just had to be avoided at all costs.

She carried on with her work, wishing she could have a drink to wash away the salty tang in her mouth. He finished the paper and left without a word. Sometime later, Giles came in.

"I see you've had a mouthful," he observed wryly.

There was no point denying it, embarrassing though it was. "How do you know?"

"You've got a splash of come on your cheek." She wiped it off. "Anyway, time to get changed. You've got an interview on the Monday Match Review tonight."

So, a few hours later, Nicky stepped into the television studio. She was elegantly dressed in a smart blouse, slacks and high heels. As last week, the outfit showed her at her very best, but the clothes were not hers and she wondered when she would next be able to wear things that actually belonged to her. Underneath her clothes, her padlock nestled comfortably in her panties. Comfortably!

"It's the same conditions as before," Giles told her on the way. "Answer all questions honestly, truthfully and fully. Don't hold anything back. One change, though: Mr. Thornton has lifted the ban on you appearing in the nude, so they'll strip you off at some point."

So I'm to be naked again, thought Nicky sadly. Between the match last Saturday and the TV highlights on Sunday, is there anybody in this city who hasn't seen me in my birthday suit? But she knew that wouldn't make it a lot easier.

It was the same interviewer as before, Samantha Dodds, but this time it was in front of a small but daunting live audience. As Nicky waited in the wings, the blonde hostess introduced her. "Last Wednesday we interviewed a fresh new girl to the arena, who was waiting for her debut match. Now let's see what she made of her first match. Please welcome Nicky Nipples!"

To cued applause from the forty or so studio audience, Nicky walked out onto the stage and settled into the interviewee's chair, feeling extremely self-conscious.

"You're still in one piece then," observed Samantha brightly.

"Just about," replied Nicky a lot less enthusiastically.

"Was it as bad as you expected?"

"It was awful," Nicky said with feeling. "Indescribable," she added, hoping that would put Samantha off that line of questioning.

It didn't. "Last week we were wondering which aspect you would find most difficult, the nudity or the pain," Samantha said. "With hindsight now, which was it?"

"They were both dreadful," said Nicky, but Samantha said nothing and she knew she would have to elaborate. "At first, it was the nudity. You can't imagine what it's like to have every inch of your body on show in front of so many leering men - unless you've been in that situation yourself?" She looked pointedly at Samantha, trying to deflect attention onto the interviewer.

"Why would I have been?" responded the blonde archly. "I'm not a slave."

That crushing retort suggested that Nicky was somehow inferior. After all, it was not her fault she had been kidnapped and brought to this terrible city.

"So at first it was the nudity," prompted Samantha. "But there were times when you forgot about that, weren't there?"

"Sometimes, when I was being tortured ... the pain makes you forget everything else."

"Well, perhaps not just then; there were one or two other things that made you forget as well. Let's have a look at a few highlights."

A large telescreen flickered into life. Nicky blushed as she saw herself come into view. She was stepping up onto the dais at the start of Saturday's match, still wearing her light summer dress. She heard again the cheers and wolf whistles from the arena crows as she reluctantly pulled the dress off to stand stark naked. Nicky blushed as she realised that the studio audience and those watching elsewhere could now see her naked on film once more. Then the scene shifted to a brief glimpse of the nude run; then of her standing with weights hanging from her boobs; and then there was cruel laughter from the studio audience at the sight of her and Katie standing bow-legged, a heavy beam between their legs as they waddled down the track in an undignified manner, carrying the beam by their excruciatingly stretched pussy lips.

"But then, on the other hand ..." murmured Samantha.

The scene shifted again, to Nicky tied face down with legs spread and a dildo pumping up between her legs. The camera shifted again to her face, mouth agape, breathing hard, perspiring. It was very clear that she was strongly aroused. The microphone picked up the stentorious sound of her breathing as she reached orgasm. The sound echoed around the studio as Nicky sat, flushing hot with shame.

"It wasn't all work and no play," observed Samantha as the scene faded.

"I had to do it," protested Nicky hoarsely. "That event ... we were being marked on the number of times we ... it was that or having the cane at the end ... and having half the crowd ... on me."

"Of course," said Samantha, clearly suggesting that Nicky was spinning a yarn, which she was not. "Anyway, we've seen your hot little body on action on the screen. Perhaps you'd like to show it us in the flesh?"

No, Nicky thought, I would not, but she had no choice. The order was as clear as if Samantha had barked the word "strip!" at her, except this was worse because it suggested she didn't mind doing it.

Nervously, Nicky stood up. Once again she was going to have to make herself naked so that these people could enjoy the sight of her body and her discomfiture. She slipped her high-heeled shoes off and began to unbutton her blouse. She pulled the ends out of her trousers and slipped it off her shoulders. The trousers were unbuttoned and she lowered them and stepped out, leaving them in a crumpled heap on the floor with her blouse and shoes. She was now reduced to bra and panties. It was perhaps no worse than being on the beach in a bikini, although she was not the bikini-wearing type: but she was not allowed to stop there. Reaching behind her back, she unclipped the bra and let it fall from her shoulders, then dug her thumbs into the waistband of the panties and pushed them down. She sat back in her chair stark naked, blushing furiously. At first she sat with legs pressed close together and an arm across her young chest, but a glare from Samantha warned her against this. Hating everything, Nicky let her arm drop and opened her legs. Her padlock nestled between her thighs and she became aware that her nipple and labia rings and the padlock were a particularly embarrassing indication of her enforced slavery.

"Not bad," said Samantha. Nicky didn't reply. The interviewer moved on. "You didn't manage to avoid the cane altogether on Saturday, did you?"

"No," said Nicky shortly.

"Let's have a look."

Nicky didn't move for a moment, then angrily got up, turned and bent over the chair, thrusting her welted bottom out at the audience and the camera, even more embarrassed than ever. Only when Samantha gave a quiet word did she resume her sitting position.

"It's good to see that Mr. Thornton takes the traditional care to ensure his young ladies remain virtuous when not on duty," Samantha observed.

Nicky looked down at the gleaming golden padlock resting between her thighs. Sat naked in a television studio, virtuous was not quite the word she would have used.

"How are you adjusting to being curtailed in that department?"

“As I don’t have a social life, it doesn’t really make much difference,” replied Nicky bitterly.

“But you agree that your little honey box should be reserved for your owner and whoever he sees fit?”

“I don’t have any choice, do I?”

“Would you rather be out on the town being a slut every night?”

“No, of course not. But ... “ she wondered if she dared say anything. Anger and humiliation defeated caution, although she chose her words carefully. “I didn’t choose to be a slave. And slavery isn’t morally right.” She wanted to say that she had been kidnapped, but thought that was unwise.

“Well, that might be a topic for our weekly debating show some time.”

“Could I appear on that?”

“Of course not, silly, they wouldn’t have a slave on a debate. Who’d be interested on your views on moral issues? Now, getting back to the subject in hand, has your owner unlocked you for use since the weekend?”

Nicky coloured. “No,” she managed. Samantha raised that eyebrow again. Oh God, thought Nicky, I’m not going to have to admit to ... but yes, she was. Giles was watching and would report the omission; possibly Samantha had even been briefed on it. “But I had to ... he made me ... suck him,” she finally blurted out.

There was a ripple of amusement among the audience. If only the earth would open up and swallow me, Nicky thought!

"There you are, you see, that's a much more productive use of your mouth than speaking in a debate," Samantha said cattily. "Well, are you looking forward to next Saturday's match?"

Nicky had been desperately trying not to think about having to endure another match. "I don't know anything about it," she said truthfully.

"Well, I'm sure there will be a big crowd again for your home debut," Samantha said. "Thank you, Nicky Nipples!"

Dismissed, Nicky walked off naked with her clothes in her hand. She dressed in the wings and went home, where several more hours of domestic chores awaited her before she could turn in for the night.

CHAPTER FOUR
Narrator

Days passed. Saturday grew closer and closer and Nicky's feelings of trapped dread grew worse. She worked long and hard hours at her domestic chores, doing even more than she was required to: after all, the alternative was to be lying in her room thinking about the forthcoming weekend.

The day came. All her bruises and marks from last weekend had gone, just in time for her to get a fresh load. This time her team was 'at home'. She was paired with the other two girls, with Katie and Gemma on the reserve bench. Once more Nicky stood up on the dais in front of a packed crowd and stripped naked. It was only marginally easier to do than last week. Once more the events were hard, painful, humiliating and hateful. Once more Nicky just had to win, to avoid the dreadful caning and crowd rape the losers would suffer. Her team-mates were less spirited than Katie or even Gemma and certainly lacked Katie's athleticism; but Nicky drove them on, cajoling, leading from the front. Fortunately the opposition was weaker than last week, another team from near the bottom of the table. It was close, but they edged it 5-4, which meant that Nicky trudged wearily home with another twenty cane marks decorating her throbbing ass.

Another week passed, thankfully without any more television interviews. There was however an 'invitation' to Mr. Thornton's bedroom one evening. Nicky went, her padlock was removed and she ‘did her duty’. It was not pleasant, to say the least; but she cooperated. Still she looked for a way out of all this. There wasn’t one.

On the next match, she was reunited with Katie and Gemma. Girls in the team were usually fielded by rotation, but that was down to the owner and he seemed to want to field Nicky every match, so that was that. Certainly it was drawing attention to her, as coverage in the local newspaper and Match Of The Day indicated, plus growing crowds for each game. None of that was particularly welcome news for Nicky. Once again she was naked before the crowd, sweating and suffering for their entertainment. At least with Katie there was a bond of competitive determination and courage and Gemma wasn’t too bad either; but the opposition was good. Very good, currently placed third. Nicky did her absolute best, an almost superhuman effort. Katie put in a similar one, less for herself than for her friend. But the other team were brave as well and fit and strong.

Nicky stood with Katie and Gemma, bruised, exhausted, dejected, feeling doomed. They had lost 5-4 on the last event. Already the two other girls in their squad were stripping off and being put into the rape racks.

“You’ll get by,” Katie said, putting an arm around Nicky’s sweaty shoulders. “It doesn’t last forever.”

“I think it’s you they want for the stirrups,” Gemma said gently.

There had never been any real doubt about that. Gemma’s bush was close to being back to full growth, although Katie still only exhibited stubble, but Nicky was the one they wanted. A steward had appeared ominously at her side and took her bare arm to march her up to the platform. Nicky pulled her arm free, determined to go under her own steam. He allowed her that. She climbed sadly onto the platform and sat in the chair. There were stirrups to either side and she placed one of her thighs in each of the two holders, acutely aware of the way in which this left her open; but then the steward pulled a lever and the stirrups swung a whole lot wider, leaving her legs far wider still. Nicky gasped at the sheer shame of it.

A geek approached. That was the only way to describe him: a feeble little man, bespectacled and slope-shouldered, with a face only his mother could have loved. Evidently he had won a prize in the raffle: the right to shave her. He looked thrilled at the prospect. He came right up to her and reached tentatively out to touch her thigh. Nicky shuddered: it was like being touched by a piece of cold, wet fish. His fingers moved up and ran through her pubic hair, sending unpleasant electric shivers through her body. Then he produced a pair of small scissors. Taking some of her pubic hair, he snapped the scissors shut. The hair came away in his hand. An expression of almost child-like glee lit up his rat-like face. He wielded the scissors again and more of Nicky's dark cherry-red pubic curls came away.

Snip, snip, snip.

When he had finished, Nicky was down to short hairs, none more than a centimetre long. They itched feverishly. Apart from trimming the edges for swimsuit purposes, Nicky had never cut her pubic hair; certainly she had never dreamed of it being removed like this. A video camera was trained on her crotch and she could see the image on a giant screen on the arena wall: everybody in the arena could see her intimacy in close-up detail. Nicky desperately wanted to close herself up, but her thighs were kept firmly apart, her legs tied to the stirrups.

Now the geek was going over her crotch with the scissors a second time, reducing the now short hairs to stubble less than half a centimetre long. Finally he produced a cordless electric razor and began to run it over her. Nicky shuddered as she felt it on her sensitive areas and winced when the longer remaining hairs were caught up in the revolving blades and yanked painfully out. The shorter hairs were sliced off with less fuss. Now the razor was making one final pass and then it was done. The geek stepped back to allow the camera a clear view and Nicky's most intimate area was displayed on the giant arena screen for all to see, bereft of the hair that had once partially shielded it. The geek stepped in again and ran his cold fishy fingers over her now smooth pudendum. The steward congratulated him on a job well done.

Nicky was released from the chair. She felt more exposed than ever, her slit totally revealed, the silver labia rings glinting in the arena spotlights. She felt that she looked like a revolting turkey done there; and there were worse torments yet to come. She was led to the stocks, where Katie and Gemma were already secured, looking miserable and fearful, if resigned. The steward opened the third set of stocks and Nicky bent over and lowered her neck and wrists into the cut-outs. There was no point in arguing, pleading or resisting. The top of the stocks came down and the steward locked them shut. Nicky was now unable to move or prevent what would happen next. Two weeks ago she had taken fifteen strokes of the cane, last week twenty; now it would be fifty. She steeled herself.

Blazing, atrocious pain. The relentless cane biting into her already battered rear again and again. Nightmare beyond belief. It was the punishment for losing. As the rattan sliced into her time after time, Nicky relived in her mind every one of the five defeats in the events. Never, never again! But in truth, it hadn't been her fault: the other team were better prepared and although Katie especially and Gemma as well had tried their best, they weren't as strong or as determined as Nicky. None of that mattered: the cane accepted no excuses, no reasons, made no slightest allowances. Fifty times it seared Nicky as she screamed her anguish, her cries mingling with those of her two young friends, no slightest concession being given.

Somehow, she survived.

The top half of the stocks was unlocked and lifted. Nicky straightened up, her ass aflame in blazing agony. Never had she known pain like this. And still her ordeal was not yet over.

Sobbing uncontrollably, Nicky stumbled towards the rape racks. Even in her ineffable agony, she was determined that she would make her own way there and submit without protest. Why this was important to her she couldn't tell, especially not at this moment: the pain made coherent thought impossible. No whys, no wherefores, no rights or wrongs came to her mind: just accept it and suffer. She lay down, gasping in fresh pain as her lacerated cheeks came into contact with the reed mat. The rest of her very considerable collection of aches and bruises faded into obscurity compared to her heavily caned rear. She opened her legs, only dimly aware that the freshly shaven crotch made her look more vulnerable than ever. She felt cold steel around her ankles as they were locked into cuffs. Now she couldn't close her legs again. Her hands were also locked into cuffs near her shoulders.

Looking to her left, she saw the two Thornton girls who had not competed today, each girl with a slavering, grunting man between her bare thighs. In either case, it was not their first and a queue of around a dozen man waiting for each girl testified that it would not be their last. If Nicky and Katie and Gemma had not lost, these girls would not be suffering this right now.

To her right, Nicky saw the sobbing figures of Katie and Gemma, secured as she herself was. A rather longer queue of men awaited each of them.

Then Nicky got up the courage to look at her own queue and felt faint.

It stretched out of sight.

The first two were already stripped from the waist down, their manhoods thickening in slobbering anticipation. Both were around thirty years old: some of those behind them were younger, others a lot older. They looked cruel and hard, the same types you might see on a football terrace. Again, the others behind them varied, some looking almost refined business types and others like road diggers: going to arena matches was not an expensive hobby. The geek was there too, about a dozen places back. Nicky didn't want to count, but she could see over twenty men in the line, with unknowably more around the corner. She cringed in her bonds, her limbs spread out and helpless, her legs held functionally wide open. She looked for mercy on the faces leering at her and saw none.

The steward allowed the first one to come forward.

"Hey baby, I've been waiting for three weeks for this," he leered at her. Nicky whimpered, unable to form coherent speech. "You sure led us a merry chase: I was beginning to think you'd never lose a match." Nicky had not dared to dream the same thing, that it would never come to this: but she had never been able to conceive of this actually happening. And yet, here she was.

He climbed on top of her. He was muscular, tattooed, rough hewn, smelling of male musk: not her type at all. As if she had a choice. She wriggled, and gasped at the fresh pain that caused in her raw bottom cheeks. He knelt down.

"We only get ten minutes each, girlie, so make it a good one," he leered. Nicky whimpered again. Then he was on top of her, his mouth crushing hers, his tongue pushing in. She was suffocating, crushed and squashed beneath his considerable weight.

Then she felt his prick nosing at her shaven haven. "Get that into you," he murmured thickly, lifting his face off hers and grabbing her full young breasts in his bear-like hands as he forced himself in. Nicky arced her back as she was entered. Her already desperately aching body felt as if he would split it in two. He was thrusting roughly, brutally into her: she felt his long pole driving deeply inside her, raping the very core of her being. His face descended again, this time burying itself into her chest: she felt his teeth biting her nipple, his tongue trying to hook itself into the (thankfully too small) silver nipple ring; but then his teeth caught the ring and pulled it, playfully for him but painfully for her, especially after the weights which had been attached to her boobs earlier in the competition.

And all the time he was thrusting, deeper and deeper, building to his climax. Suddenly he exploded into her and Nicky felt steaming hot jets of come spurting deep into her body.

"Ahhh ... ooohhhh ... get some of that, you little beauty!" he slavered.

"Uugghhhh ... ooohhhh ..." she gasped, revolted, hurting and shamed beyond measure.

For long moments he lay on her, wheezing contentedly; then a voice behind them called out.

"Hey Mac, if you've finished, there's a lot more of us waiting!"

The beast looked up towards the speaker and grinned. "Sure," he said, "but I tell you what, she's worth the wait. Hot and tight, that's what this little bitch is! Man! What a body!" He pulled himself out, his penis escaping with a faint plop. "Okay guys, who's next? She's all yours!"

Defeated, violated, beaten black and blue and still with no end to her ordeal in sight, Slave Nicky Nipples looked helplessly towards the line as the next man stepped eagerly forwards.

Nicky drifted in and out of reality.

She had lost count, but through mist-filled eyes she could still see no end to the line. Most of the rapes were mercifully short, but very intensive. Some were rough, others more gentle, almost kind except for their determination to have their way and get their sperm into her. What seemed like gallons of hot sticky semen were shot into her slot. The geek was one of the less rough, but his cold fishy hands clawed and probed her flesh. It took him almost the full ten minutes to come. One or two of the gentler ones she tried to keep for longer, to give her a few moments respite from the more brutal treatment she got from the others.

Then, at last, her tear-filled eyes saw an end to the line.

Just another twenty to go!

With terrible slowness, the line gradually shortened. Then Nicky's already low spirits sank further still as, with the queue down to just four, a group of three more men joined the back of the queue, laughing and chatting together; but there was nothing she could do about it, any more than she could wish away the man who was humping her right at that moment. Still, the line gradually shortened, with no more additions, until there was only one more waiting: and then that last one was on top of her, thrusting in; and then he was gone. It was over.

The steward stepped in and unlocked her chains. Every movement an unbelievable anguish, Nicky groaned and just rolled over, curling herself into a foetal ball. The steward left her to it.

Katie and Gemma were there. They were hurting terribly themselves, but their two queues put together had been shorter than Nicky's: the media attention and celebrity status of the newcomer, marketed assiduously by her owner irrespective of her own wishes, had resulted in massive interest. Katie and Gemma stood, numerous drops of semi-dried come on their inner thighs, bruises standing out all over their bodies, their bottoms turning purple with their weals, exhausted by their ordeals, but still in better shape than Nicky. The two naked teenagers stooped down and pulled the third to her feet, one of them under each of her shoulders, her arms draped over their own bare shoulders.

"Uuhhhh," was all Nicky could manage.

"Yeah, I know," said Gemma. "You'd have thought the other two girls would have stayed to help. Even Giles ..."

"Mr. Thornton wanted Giles for something. And as for the other two, never mind them. Can you walk, Nicky?"

The young beauty, her dark cherry-red hair dishevelled, tried and would have collapsed but for the other two holding her up. After her caning, walking had become extremely painful and difficult; now it was unbelievably worse. She felt as if she had a red-hot poker permanently up her vagina.

"Lean on us, then," said Katie, not in much better shape herself. They staggered out of the arena. Nicky was far too gone to heed the fact that she was naked on the streets of the city; but she was becoming aware that Katie and Gemma had suffered terribly as well and it was unfair that they should have to half-carry her. Somehow the strong-willed ex-karate champion dug deep into herself and forced more of her weight onto her bare feet. One of today's events had been bastinado and all three girls had welts and the soles of their feet. It was just one more cross to bear. From having her arms around her comrades to keep herself on her feet, Nicky gradually changed to having her arms around them for their mutual comfort as the three shattered girls staggered home.

CHAPTER FIVE
Nicky

I was hurting so much after that match.

I couldn't move the next day. I got hourly treatments of cream for my bruises by that young lad. He also ... well, there's no way to say this without embarrassment, but he had some ointment to put up my passage for the bruising and chafing there and he had to use his fingers to get it there, do you get my meaning? Not very nice.

I spent all day lying face down on the bed, most of the time softly crying. It wasn't just the pain, it was also what had been done to me. The crowd rape, I mean.

Monday came, but Giles saw that I was still in quite a state and he left me off the work rota. He was very kind to me during the day, regularly calling in to give me more cream treatment and the ointment between my legs. That meant his fingers had to invade me as well. He was almost apologetic about it.

On Tuesday, though, he couldn't give me any more leeway, so I was back in my maid's outfit, polishing and dusting. I have to admit that I was listless, half-hearted and unresponsive. Giles came in after a couple of hours, inspected my work, and shook his head sadly. "Your work is not good enough, slave," he said formally. "Get over my lap."

I didn't argue, not that there would have been any point in protesting anyway. I put myself over his legs, felt him flick back my short skirt and pull my knickers down to reveal my still purple and very sore bottom. Six slaps on that very tender rear hurt, a lot.

But then he sat me down and talked to me and after a while talked with me as I began to open up. It took some time, but he brought me out of it. He pointed out the story I had told him of the world karate competition; of losing the semi-final, but then coming back to win two more contests to take the bronze and therefore not giving in after a setback. Gradually, he dealt with the deeper problem: my feelings of self-revulsion and loathing after being raped by so many men. He talked to me as perhaps only one slave could do to another, explaining with conviction that it wasn't my fault, that there was nothing to be ashamed of, that it was just a slave being used, a beautiful (his word) slave whose body was a fine asset to her owner. I brought up something else that had nagged me, the fact that I had capitulated into slavery without a fight; but he countered by praising my intelligence for doing so, as resistance would have been very stupid. He also said how impressed he and many others had been by my phenomenal bravery and determination, particularly in the arena, but at other times too.

He was a silver-tongued devil. By the end of it I was, well, not happy, but my equilibrium was restored.

"Now that's all sorted," Giles said, "I haven't finished your spanking yet."

Incredibly, I actually didn't mind. I realised that he was reasserting his position as my supervisor after coming down to my level to talk to me; and he was letting me know that, although I had needed counselling, that did not excuse my sloppy work. I suppose it didn't. I mean, in their eyes it didn't. Oh, I don't really know what I mean. Anyway, I bent over, took my second six slaps, which hurt, and got back to work, determined not to let him find fault with my work again. You figure out why.

I was dreading Saturday, but it came around with inexorable inevitability. No matter how much I wanted time to stand still and the horrid day never come, it did.

My body, even my bum, was just about recovered. Only the last couple of days had been completely pain-free and now the whole thing was going to happen all over again. Or so I thought. Only once my chastity padlock had been removed and we were on our way to the arena (we were at home this week) was I told that I wasn't in the team this week. I took my place on the bench with Katie and watched as Gemma and the other two stripped for action. I had been spared!

But Katie, next to me, was still sombre and it didn't take long to figure out why. Without either me or Katie in the team, Thornton's Fillies were soon losing. If the team lost the match, all five girls in the squad, myself and Katie included, would be on the rape racks. Dressed in a very short skirt with no knickers on, I was already feeling vulnerable enough and this realisation made me feel even sicker.

The match was a rout: we lost 7-2. As the last event ended, Katie and I were beckoned to our feet. Without needing to be told, Katie was already pulling off her dress to reveal her cute elfin figure. I took my own dress off. Naked again in public! We were taken over to the rape racks and strapped in, legs secured apart. Gemma and the other two were being marched off to the stocks for their caning, while some mousy secretary girl was squirming with embarrassment nude in the stirrups as her pubic hair was shaven. Katie was showing fairly thick stubble down there now, whilst I was still bald and feeling even more exposed as a result. There was a big queue for each of us: Katie was popular with the home crowd and my queue was even longer.

I got gang-banged again. I cried a lot, which made no difference. I co-operated, to make it less painful, knowing it would be a lengthy ordeal. I had another forty or so cocks go up me, one after another. I think some were repeats from last week, but I was rarely sure. How nice a feeling is that for a young girl, to not even be sure if a man in front of her has had her before?

But I got through it; and although I was sore again the next day, my mind wasn't so badly screwed this time.

Only my body.

On the sports page of the Corvalle Gazette last week had been a rumour that I was up for sale. Naturally, I had read it with extreme interest: it was the only source of information I had.

"Nicky Nipples has been an inspiration to a struggling Thornton's Fillies team," it ran. "They've won twice through her and started to move away from the bottom of the table. It surely won't be long, then, before one of the big teams with more genuine aspirations makes a bid for her. Properly trained, she could be an asset for any team and the Downtown Slits are openly looking to strengthen their side, but the smart money is on Sutton's Slags as they chase Tibbets' Tits for the title. I expect to see Nicky's perky young boobs suffering for the cause of a different team before long."

I blushed furiously at the mention of my boobs: it was another reminder, as if any was needed, how my personal privacy had been ripped away in this perverted city. But the theme of the article soon resumed centre stage in my mind. It was so much like professional football, where players are transferred from one club to another and yet in other ways so different, not least in the fact that the competitors were forced into taking part and that, when talking of a player being sold, the newspaper meant just that. Thornton did not own a contract on me, he actually owned me. Quite literally, I could be sold.

Again like football, the income for team owners came from crowd entry fees, TV rights, merchandising and personal appearances. The last one was very different to the football analogy. Several clubs loaned their girls out as dinner companions: Tibbets' Tits had the richest share of that market, being the top side in the league. Of course, the girls' duties on such dates would emphatically involve everything. Although the Downtown Slits girls were a hard-training team, the girls also worked in the evenings as lap dancers at the Slits Nightclub; and you can guess that nightclubs in this city are not governed by the sort of restrictions British law has. To put it another way, this club would be very much hands ON.

The crowd money remained the biggest earner, though. I had gathered that attendances for Thornton's matches had gone up quite a bit since my arrival - something I could well have done without the last two weekends.

It had been inevitable that we would lose sooner or later. I knew it, no matter how hard I fought against it. But it didn't make the consequences any less easy to bear. Being shaved in public was almost as bad as the first time I had had to strip off for a match and the caning had been brutal and agony. But then, being locked, already sobbing my heart out, in the rape racks ... and just seeing the queue of men lining up for me ...

The usual situation is that out of an average crowd of two hundred, maybe half will avail themselves of the bound girls. Of the others, some are women, others can't be bothered to queue - bear in mind that there's a huge amount of slave women in this city available to men at very little or no cost - and, according to some of the girls, quite a few men go off in their trousers during high points in the match: in fact, some intend to and come with plenty of tissue paper stuffed down their pants to absorb the emissions. You can imagine how sick all that makes me feel. Anyway, that leaves around a hundred men divided between five girls, so about twenty each. That's no joke for a girl.

But with all the publicity about me, there were over three hundred at the first match we lost and they wanted me. My line stretched out of sight. The mere sight of all those slavering beasts, the front few already with trousers down and swollen dicks jutting obscenely out, made me want to die with both shame and fear. When the first one climbed onto me, I just felt sick to the pit of my stomach. By the time the fifth started on me, I felt like a worthless slut of a slave. When the tenth got going, I was physically hurting. I lost count soon after that.

Giles said there were eighty in the line to start with. Eighty! I think some then decided to go for one of the others rather than wait for ages, especially as they weren't allowed as much time each. I don't know how many it was in the end: but I think I was there for around five hours and I couldn't walk afterwards. The second week, it was around fifty men, which wasn't much better.

It was now Tuesday and I was back to polishing and cleaning in my maid's outfit, but I was still stiff and sore. The bigger impact, however, had been mentally. My life before I was captured seemed even more distant now, a life I could never go back to no matter how much I wanted to. Another awful Rubicon had been passed.

Giles appeared. This was highly unusual. It was around three o'clock in the afternoon and I was normally made to work until ten in the evening, and Giles normally only appeared to dismiss me to me tea and then take me to fresh tasks afterwards.

"How are you feeling?" he asked, genuinely. He was always strict with me, but not unkind. It was a small but appreciated mercy.

It would have been easy to wail about my situation, but it wouldn't get me anywhere and it just isn't my nature. "I'll be all right," I said, not wanting to dwell on the nature and reason for my soreness. "But I'm struggling to get my work done in time. Please ... if I haven't finished, can I be given some extra time tonight?" It would mean, I estimated, working until midnight at least, but the alternative was punishment of a much more painful type if I didn't finish my tasks - and do them very thoroughly. No slacking was allowed.

"That may be irrelevant," he said. "Go to your room and make yourself look your very best. John Sutton is here."

John Sutton!

"Wh-what shall I wear?"

"Nothing, of course. Go!"

John Sutton, I reflected as I showered, brushed my hair, applied light touches of makeup and perfume and polished my chastity lock. He owned Sutton's Slags, currently second in the league and the only team with a realistic hope of catching Tibbets' Tits: in general, a team very much on the up, hugely ambitious to challenge the Tits' dominance of the league. He could only be here to negotiate about buying me for his team, as the newspaper had speculated. Could I hack it in a team of that quality?

It may seem strange to you that I would be so preoccupied with the ins and outs of the league, given my overall predicament. But you only have to reflect on what I had suffered three days before as part of a losing team to understand how important winning is to arena girls. My bottom still ached from the cane and the marks were very visible, but the massive crowd rape, my second in eight days, had been even worse.

My preparations complete, I waited nervously for Giles to collect me. I was, as instructed, naked. I can always tell when I'm nude now. There's the greater freedom of movement, the slight feel of the air moving around my bare body - rather more since my shaving - but most of all the slight tugging sensation of my chastity lock hanging from my sex lips, unsupported by my knickers.

Giles came, looked me over very quickly and led me off. He's seen me naked often enough now, but it's still not entirely comfortable for me. I think it's because I'm forced into it.

"Needless to say," Giles told me as we walked along, "Mister Thornton will not be too happy if he doesn't get a good price for you." The implied threat was frightening, but it was in my own interests to be transferred. If a girl must be in the arena, it's far better to be with a winning team.

"Ah, here she is," said Thornton to his guest as I was led into the lounge. Without needing to be told, I stood stiff and straight and allowed them to inspect my naked charms: whether I liked it or not, and I didn't, I had no choice. It was better to be gawped at than punished - especially right now, both because I was still so sore from the weekend and in view of the importance of this meeting.

Trying not to be obvious, I studied Sutton as his eyes roved over my body. He was older than Thornton, maybe nudging sixty, and looked every inch the successful, ruthless businessman. I shuddered to think what being owned by him would mean and yet Thornton had dominated me thoroughly as well. John Sutton would take what he wanted from me, I knew with a shudder of fear. But then, didn't everybody around here?

Sutton got up and came over to me and I steeled myself not to flinch if he began pawing me: Thornton would have me thrashed severely if I messed this sale up.

"She's got a great body," my owner was saying enthusiastically. "Just turned eighteen, a perfect age for an arena girl. Nice tits, very firm, good muscle tone."

"Not bad, not bad," admitted Sutton as he wandered slowly around me and I fought to keep myself from cringing with embarrassment and humiliation. "But pretty girls can be bought for ten a penny in the market."

"But you've seen this one's performances in the arena! When did you last see a girl that good?"

Sutton nodded easily. "Yes, she's got potential. Still, forty thousand is a high price."

I fought to keep my face impassive. Forty thousand! Thornton had bought me for eight. My parents, of course, would have paid every penny they had, around three times this, to buy my freedom, but they were not here to bid.

"That should add to her value," Thornton pointed out. "A league record fee for a near novice and not far short of the transfer record for an established player: should add a few to your attendance level. And most importantly, she could help you win the league from the Tits; if not this season, certainly next year."

Sutton nodded. I'd read that winning the league title was very important to him: he'd run the Slags team for several years as a mid-table outfit, but now he had retired from serious business and decided to throw his energies and money into building a team to rival the Tits. Did he see me as part of that team? And if so, could I live up to it? Each match was a nightmare torment; the effort and endurance of torment needed to win was terrible.

"On the other hand," Sutton countered, "she's been scalped. That lowers her value somewhat."

I went very red: I could feel my cheeks burning. It wasn't just the attention being drawn to my now bald crotch and totally exposed and vulnerable sex lips, or vulnerable if it had not been for the small, gleaming golden padlock which kept those lips together; but also, it was the fact that an arena girl with a shaved pussy would also have been through a crowd rape. For weeks to come, my baldness, or later stubble, down there would tell everybody what had happened to me.

"It wasn't her fault the team lost," Thornton said defensively.

"Oh, I agree, I saw the match. Those other dogs you've got didn't pull their weight."

To know that I had received that dreadful caning, had my crotch shaved in public and had been raped by sixty or seventy men as a punishment for something that was not my fault was a bitter pill. I clenched my fists silently at my sides and fought to remain impassive.

"It's actually more of a shame she wasn't a virgin on arrival," Thornton observed. My already furious blushing deepened. I was wondering if it was possible to be any more humiliated than this.

Sutton smiled, allowing Thornton's diversion to proceed. "True," he mused, and an aged finger reached out and stroked my trembling breast. "You're a very naughty girl," he told me, almost the first time he had spoken to me. "Your lustful behaviour before your acquisition has cost your owner quite a bit of money."

To be told off for that, when they had made me do so many disgusting things! It just wasn't fair; and yet I had no choice but to go along with it. "Sorry, Master," I said, trying to sound sincere.

"Did you punish her for that?" he asked Thornton, once again acting as if I wasn't there.

"No," said the other man. "After all, she couldn't have known that she'd end up here."

How true that was! Never in my wildest nightmares could I have imagined that a place like this even existed, let alone that I would be a victim of it. My nightmares in those naïve, carefree days before all this used to be about doing badly in a major tournament, or worst of all not making the team for the World Championships.

Actually, to be precise, my worst nightmare was losing my place to my one hated rival, Claire Sanderson. I'm a pretty easy-going person and not the sort to make enemies, but she was the one exception. She and I got into a huge row because she accused me of making a play for a boy she had her eye on. It was very public and very embarrassing - at least by the standards of my life in those pre-slavery days - and made worse by the fact that it was totally untrue: I wasn't interested in him in the slightest.

Thank God Claire Sanderson can't see me now! She always reckoned I was trying to lead the boys on by dressing modestly, while she wore revealing, skimpy outfits. She wouldn't believe her eyes if she saw me standing naked in front of two men, my nipples and labia pierced and ringed, my pubic hair freshly shaved off, while they discuss selling me. I'm not sure I believe it sometimes. I know I don't want to believe it.

Nobody from my old life could possibly guess the awful price I paid for winning that World Championships medal. They knew the price I paid then, the dedication, the long hours of training and self-sacrifice; but not the price I'm paying now, because if I hadn't gone to that World Championships, I wouldn't be here now. And yet ... I refuse to regret it. If I did that, my life would stop having any meaning. And however terrible things are, I just don't regret it. When I lie in bed on a Saturday night, every inch of my body on fire with pain from that day's match and the memory of the shame and humiliation of it all burning just as badly, I look up at that medal in its frame and I feel proud that I'm taking the punishment for winning it without complaining.

That Saturday of the first defeat had been the worst, with that brutal caning on top of everything else and the pain between my legs and the degradation of it all and the very public announcement and reminder of what had happened for weeks to come by the shaving of me down there, in addition to the extra exposure of me that brought. But do you know, I still looked up at that medal and didn't regret it. I also thought of Vic, my old coach. He taught me so much, not just about karate but about attitude and right and wrong and so much else. He also worked so hard to help me and I really respected him. I wonder if he would be proud of me for taking all this on the chin.

Really, if there's one person from my old life I could almost bear to see me now, it's him. I think he would be proud of me. Of course, he'd see me naked and all the rest of it. Thinking about it, if we lost he'd have the right to join the queue for me. But then, on Saturday I'd had a lot of much worse men than him inside me. A lot worse.

"We're waiting, slave."

A feeling of cold dread shot up my spine as I realised that they had said something to me and I had missed it, lost in my thoughts. What had they said? A question, a command? I had no way of knowing. I would have to confess. I knew I would suffer for this indiscretion later.

"M-Master, I'm very, very sorry," I began. "I didn't hear ..."

"She's usually pretty attentive," said Thornton apologetically to Sutton. "What were you thinking about that was so important, wretch?"

I was expected to bare my soul just as much as I had to bare my body. "I was thinking about last weekend's match, master," I said: it was partially true. "I didn't like losing." I thought this was what Sutton would want to hear.

"You didn't like losing in general, or your backside and pussy didn't like the consequences?" Sutton asked.

"Both, Master," I replied truthfully. It would be foolish to indulge in a blatant and unnecessary lie about the latter.

Sutton turned to Thornton. "Would you leave us alone for a few minutes?"

Thornton nodded and left without looking at me. He didn't need to send any coded glances: I knew I had to sell myself as much as possible to Sutton. But in any case, it was in my interests to do so: Sutton's Slags lost a lot less often than Thornton's Fillies.

Sutton relaxed in his chair and regarded me. I was suddenly actually grateful for the little golden lock which hung from my slightly stretched pussy lips: a naked girl who has no rights to decline sexual intercourse with a man learns that a chastity device is as much a blessing as a restriction. My labia were beginning to ache just a little, as they usually did when I stood with my lock unsupported for any length of time, but I was glad of the lock, nevertheless. Of course, if he did buy me, he would have full access to me. I tried to put that from my mind. In any case, whoever owned me had that.

"Your owner has put a price of forty thousand pounds on you," he mused at last. "Are you worth that, do you think?"

It was a pittance to pay for total control of a young life and yet I knew it was a huge price for a slave in this land. "I don't know, Master," I said cautiously. "I mean, I don't know the economics of it; but if it's worth that to get a player who can help your team win matches, then yes. I want to win."

"No girl in the arena wants to lose. The forfeits see to that. I'm looking for more than that. I need girls who want to win the league, not just to avoid punishment but because they want to win."

"I'm a natural competitor, Master," I said. "If you've seen my file, you'll know that."

For a long moment he looked at me. I wondered if I should have said more; but then he went to the door and called my owner back in.

"Forty thousand, sold as seen," Sutton said to my owner. "I'll send somebody round to collect her first thing in the morning."

He offered his hand, not to me but to Thornton and they shook on the deal. I now belonged to a new owner.

Giles took me back to my dusting and polishing chores. He didn't send me to get dressed first: no point, really. Besides, as he pointed out, I had to make up for the time lost during my interview. It was a totally moot point whether this was fair: it was the way it would be whatever I thought. Fortunately, much of the work could be done one-handed, so I was able to use my other hand to cup my chastity lock and relieve the slight but insistent pressure on my sex.

Although I always had to work hard, the work was mundane enough that my mind could wander. I had been sold: tomorrow I would be leaving this place. There wasn't much I would miss: certainly not the drudgery work. There was a degree of camaraderie amongst the girls because of what we have endured together, but as we were kept separated except at matches I hadn't really been able to get to know them. I had a lot of time for Katie, quite a bit for Gemma, less so for the other two; but I only ever saw them at matches or in passing, so I hadn't established any real friendship with them, just the bond of slaves suffering together: a substantial bond in some ways, but limited in many others.

It occurred to me that the person I would miss most was Giles. He was strict with me and carried out Thornton's instructions about me to the letter and without the slightest mercy and yet he had been kind, thoughtful and had helped me through some of the worst things. I should thank him before I go, I mused: a kiss and a cuddle and I could buy him a present like some chocolates or whiskey. My musing came to an abrupt halt as I realised the stupidity of that last bit. I was a slave: I had no money, quite conceivably never would have again, and could not buy anyone anything. All I had to offer was me, my body; but as I stood there, one hand polishing a mirror whilst the other cupped that little golden padlock and supported it so that the weight wasn't pulling on my sensitive areas, I was reminded that I couldn't even offer that: my own sexual favours were no longer considered mine to give. At least, not without permission.

Then I would ask for permission.

Don't ask me why. I've thought about that quite a bit since then. It was the first time, you see, as a slave, that I had volunteered to have sex. I did genuinely want to thank Giles, and just giving him a kiss seemed so feeble in view of, well, everything else that goes on around here. But there were other motivations too. After all that forced sex, I think I wanted to do it at least once just because I wanted to: almost a minor act of rebellion, to prove to myself that I still had some free will. I also had to admit to myself that having sex was no longer the big deal it had been before I had been brought here: pre-abduction, only two men had been intimate with me, but after the last two weekends, the length of that list had been multiplied by a factor of fifty at least. What difference would another one make? But I was kidding myself on that point: it did make a difference. Nevertheless, I was still going to do it; if, that is, I was given permission.

I knew the layout of the house and where people tended to be pretty well these days. Leaving my cleaning duties (and aware that I was risking punishment for doing so), I went to Thornton's study and knocked nervously on the door. When his voice boomed out "come in," I suddenly got very nervous about the whole thing: but it was too late now. In I went.

He showed no surprise whatsoever at the entry of a stark naked eighteen year-old girl; such is the bizarre nature of life around here. I put my arms behind me, keeping my body exposed to him: I wouldn't dare do anything else. The little golden padlock swung gently between my legs, tugging slightly on my labia.

This man had accepted me from my kidnappers and legitimised their abduction of me. He had had sex with me three times, each time without my consent, or at least with my cooperation given under duress and threat. He had forced me to strip naked in the arena in front of hundreds of people, mostly men, and put me through cruel tortures and humiliations there for the entertainment of the depraved audience and his financial profit. Now he had sold me to another ruthless, evil man. I hated him: but I would never dare do anything about it, never dare even admit it. It was unwise to even dwell on it to myself in case I let my feelings show, or worse do something I would later be made to regret beyond belief.

"Yes, slave?" He could not even be bothered to use my name.

It suddenly occurred to me just how embarrassing this was going to be. It was bad enough having to appear nude before him, but to say what I wanted to do, and to tacitly admit that I required his permission to do it, was going to be awful. I took a deep breath.

"Master, as I'm leaving tomorrow" - put like that, it sounded as if it was by my choice - "and Giles has been so helpful to me" - I tried not to think of the times when he had taken a belt to me or how he had made me work so hard for long hours, and of course he had abetted keeping me in captivity - "that I'd like to, well, do something to say thank you to him."

"So? I don't have a problem with that."

There was an awkward pause. He was clearly going to make me spell it out to him. I took the plunge. "Could you ... would you be prepared to unlock me ... so I can ... thank him ... thoroughly?"

He didn't show any sign of surprise; but after a moment an amused look came into his eye as he regarded me. "Are you blushing, girl?"

"Y-yes, Master," I said in some confusion. Everything had become so bizarre in my life. Just six weeks ago it had all been perfectly normal: I could never have believed it would change to all this. Just imagine: I was standing, stark naked, in front of a middle-aged man. My nipples were pierced and each now sported a little silver ring, rings whose main purpose was to facilitate extremely unpleasant torment on me. My pussy was freshly shaved, so that it was as bald as it had been when I was about twelve. My very exposed sex lips also had two silver rings and again their main purpose was to help cause me pain; but also they were currently pulled together by that little golden padlock which, whilst it did not stop me being molested, did prevent me from being penetrated. The padlock hung down ever so slightly between my legs, uncomfortably stretching my lips just a little bit. Just bear in mind that I don't have the key to that padlock and what that says about my situation. If you looked at my behind, which was as much on show as the rest of me, you would see the fading but unmistakeable marks of a caning; and I was still walking stiffly as a result of being fucked - there is no other word for it - by around sixty - yes, sixty - men, all strangers, a few days ago. I was standing here asking if the holder of the key to that padlock would mind unlocking me for an hour so that I could go with another man a good deal older than me. If you had told me all that six weeks ago I would have thought you to be totally crazy.

"So you want to give young Giles a taste of your honey box to say thank you?"

'Young' Giles was around forty; I was eighteen. "Yes, Master."

"Hmm. You're still my property until tomorrow morning, even if the cheque's already deposited in the bank." He considered for a moment and I realised that he might refuse the request. If he did, I would have to accept it. A feeling of total, utter helplessness came over me. "In any case," he added, "how is it you're talking about rewarding Giles but not me? I'm the one who bought you and set you on the road to fame and fortune - well, fame anyway."

Fame, of a very unwanted sort, was right: he had exposed my blushing body to hundreds of men for each of the last four weeks in the arena. Thousands more would have seen it, and the vile things I'd been made to do, on the television highlights programme. And last Saturday some sixty men had got to know me even more intimately. I felt as if every flimsiest veil of privacy had been ripped brutally away from me.

However, I didn't have time to reflect on that right now. I realised that I'd dropped myself in it. A severe punishment could be coming my way if I didn't talk my way out of this; and however much it sickened me, there was only one route out.

"I was going to leave the best till last, Master," I said with an attempt at coy invitation; "and I thought you'd have me anyway if you wanted me a- and you know I always want to please you if I can." Bitterness welled briefly inside me as I said these words to the man who had dragged me down so low, but it was the only way to avoid excruciating punishment. With an effort, I pushed those feelings down. They were dangerous.

He laughed. "You're a silver-tongued devil, Miss Nipples. You're right, you'll be spending tonight with me, your last duty to me. And I was going to give you to Giles anyway. Come here and let me see if I can find that key."

I moved over to within easy reach of him. So Giles would have had access to me anyway. I could have spared myself this. But no, I had made the gesture to Giles. I felt Thornton's hands slipping between my thighs - I would feel that a lot more tonight - and there was a faint click as the lock turned. The slight weight eased from my crotch and the bar of the lock slipped out of my rings. I suddenly felt much more vulnerable: I could be had now and you have to remember that there is no rape law here to protect me. Only citizens enjoy the rights of the law: slaves have nothing.

"Tell Giles he can have an hour off, no, two hours." He patted my bottom like an indulgent dirty uncle. "Off you go and give him a good time."

CHAPTER SIX
Nicky

The following morning, I stood waiting to be collected, just outside the doorway to Thornton's mansion. That in itself was very embarrassing, because I was stark naked. Even my padlock had been removed: apparently I had been "sold as seen". People were walking by and looked up. Nobody appeared particularly surprised by my nudity, nor should they be: naked slave girls were common enough in this city. That didn't make me feel any better, though, because this naked slave girl was me.

I was just a little bit concerned at being without my padlock. On the induction video, it had been explained that the law clearly specified that nobody may have sex with a slave without their owner's permission. However, it had also been added that it was a standard convention that, if a man sent his slave out naked onto the streets, unless she is wearing a chastity device she is considered available. Fortunately. I was not actually on the street, but on private property, even though I was in full view. That, apparently, made the difference. It didn't do much for my nerves, though.

Giles had come and kissed me goodbye. He had been very sweet. I have to confess that I'd actually enjoyed my stint with him last night. I wasn't expecting to: he was much older than me and not particularly handsome or dashing and I'd done it just because I felt I owed him something and it was the only way I could repay him; but deep down I think I had wanted to re-establish my right to choose. Of course I didn't have that right: I'd had to go and ask permission, and actually so had he. But even so I felt I'd made just a tiny step towards free will. Anyway, he'd been kind and gentle, and it was a long while since I'd felt that sort of consideration.

Now, very nervously, I was waiting to be claimed by my new owner. You can have no idea how scared that made me.

I did have one possession: my world karate medal, still mounted in its frame, in a little carrier bag by my side. That also made me nervous: my new owner could take it and throw it in a rubbish bin if he felt like it. That would have broken my heart: that medal had cost me my freedom and losing it would render that sacrifice meaningless. I would beg my new master to let me keep it; but whether that would have any effect remained to be seen.

A young man came up the steps and looked at me. I blushed furiously: when I say he looked at me, I mean he had a good, undisguised look at everything. He was maybe twenty or so and quite dishy. I'm not sure whether that made it worse than if he had been fat and fifty.

"You Nicky Nipples?" he asked.

"Yes, sir," I said meekly.

He turned from me and knocked on the door. Giles answered it and handed him some documents. I realise that those documents were my ownership certificate and the invoice for my sale. It's strange, to see yourself reduced to just two pieces of paper.

"This young man, Ben, is in the employ of your new owner," Giles said to me. "Go with him and good luck for the future."

"Does she need leashing?" Ben asked Giles.

"No, she's quite tame," Giles replied. Ben nodded and Giles disappeared with a final wink to me. The young man started down the steps. I followed him.

Walking naked down the fairly busy street was quite an experience and not a very pleasant one. I'd done it once before, on the way back from my third match, the first time I'd been crowd-raped, but I think it was safe to say that I'd had other things on my mind then. Today there was nothing to distract me from the display I was giving. All right, so I go naked in the arena, but on the street it's different. The lookers are closer, for one thing.

"Hey, isn't that Nicky Nipples?"

A group of young men had spotted me. I was hoping that Ben would hurry on, but instead he stopped. The young men looked at me expectantly.

"Yes," I said quietly, "I'm Nicky Nipples."

"Thought I recognised those tits," the one said and there was laughter from the group. I blushed furiously.

"Hey, the papers and TV reckon you might be transferred soon," another ventured. "Any truth in that?"

"I've been sold today," I confirmed, "to Sutton's Slags."

"Cool," said another. "I'm a Sutton fan."

"I might become one if they've got you in the team," the first one said. "I've watched your matches on TV: you're good."

"Thank you, sir." Well, what else could I say?

"Let's have a feel of that bum!"

I felt a hand grasp my nether cheeks. "Please," I begged.. Another hand was on my boobs now. I looked to Ben for help, but he just watched patiently. For a minute or two I was groped, openly in the street without anyone turning a hair, then fortunately they got bored and moved on. I breathed a massive sigh of relief. Ben moved on, making a comment about me having a fan club.

We arrived at the registry office. Unlike my previous encounter with Mr. Anston, this time I was stark naked. Papers were exchanged. I was not asked to sign anything: as a slave, my signature no longer had any validity in this country.

We went on to Sutton's base, a big house right on the edge of the city's suburbs, with a good view of the sea. I looked longingly down towards the beach, but such things were no longer for me. Inside, I was shown to a room, where I was allowed to hang my framed medal. It was a much nicer room than at Thornton's. Then I was taken to meet the other squad members. Clearly, the regime here was very different than with my previous team.

The four girls were all very lovely, but also clearly extremely fit and spirited. They looked around my own age or a few years older. They all wore bras and knickers, but I noted the imprint of a padlock in each pair of knicks. A similar set was found for me and a new padlock. It was a relief to be dressed again; even if, before my kidnapping, I wouldn't have considered this as being dressed in mixed company.

The girls made it plain, without being aggressive, that I would be expected to pull my weight. I assured them that I would: I was so relieved to be away from Thornton's.

It was time for the girls' daily gym session. I was given a pair of good quality trainers and socks - I felt slightly ridiculous dressed in only underwear and trainers - and we were taken to a well-equipped, air-conditioned gym at the rear of the house. Each of us had to lower her panties to have our padlocks removed and then we were put to work. A male trainer supervised us, paying particular attention to me. I've done gym training before as part of my karate training, but this programme was really strenuous. That suited me just fine: I like to work up a sweat. He carried a broad strap and I got thwacked with it a few times for encouragement. It stung but, well, it made me work even harder. The other girls got strapped from time to time as well, even though they were working extremely hard.

By the end of the session, we were all dripping in sweat. After dropping our soaked undies in a laundry bin, we went into a sauna and then a communal shower. There was an excellent camaraderie between the girls and they soon included me, although it was made clear that I was still on trial. I accepted that: given that these girls could face a crowd rape, a lengthy caning and the loss of their chance of catching Tibbet's Tits for the league title if I cost them a match, it was fair enough.

Much of the day was spent in training of one sort or another. Various skills, some of them quite bizarre (remember the balloon popping with needles taped to tits from one match?) were practised. We'd been provided with fresh bras and panties, which we had to remove only when needed (such as for the balloon popping).

During supervised physical training, our padlocks were left off, but were put on for lunch and at other times. We were actually served lunch, a luxury I had long forgotten and it was good food, healthy and tasty. Sutton had several other slaves, male and female, for domestic work: I would not be spending long hours dusting and cleaning again. After lunch we had an hour for nude sunbathing on the lawn to improve our tans, then it was onto other training. We also had a massage each from our trainer. I had to go nude for that, but, well, he was very dishy and actually quite professional about it. I'd already gathered from the girls that they all fancied him like mad and I was quite happy to join them in that. Unfortunately I had also been told that we were kept celibate during the season, to keep us hot for the orgasm event in the matches. Out of season, well, he was apparently one of several who had sex rights over us without needing to ask specific permission of Mr. Sutton. The other girls were all quite happy about that as well and I was already wondering if I wouldn't be too outraged about it either.

One thing I was acutely embarrassed about was that I was the only one with a shaved delta. It was a while since these girls had lost a match and the last girl to be shaved had more or less grown her thatch back now. They didn't think any the less of me for it: they knew the defeat had not been my fault. Still, it was embarrassing. Very, very faint signs of stubble were just starting to show and I wished they would hurry up and sprout more fully.

During the massage, the trainer, whose name was Ian, informed me that I would be starting a karate club the next week to teach the girls some combat skills. My apparently unique way of winning whipping matches had not gone unnoticed and it could also be used for other optional events. It sounded an interesting challenge: I had never instructed before.

In the evening we were allowed to relax and socialise. I was very tired, but the day had been, once I got here at least, actually quite enjoyable. The evening was nice, too: as I got to know the girls, I realised they were very likeable as well as really spirited. The camaraderie I had noticed was really strong and there was also a fierce sense of honour between them which I liked too. We had lots of facilities: computer games, internet access (but with no email!), cards, board games, TV and radio and plenty of music CDs. We gambled with dice for forfeits and had riotous fun. By the end of the day, I had almost forgotten that I was a slave. Even my padlock didn't bother me.

The next day, Thursday, was much the same, except that the training was sufficiently varied to keep it interesting. Friday, however, was rest day, the day before a match. A tension descended on all of us: tomorrow would be an ordeal, for three of us at least. The team to take part was announced: I was not in it. Ian explained that they wanted me to have more training before fielding me. It seemed sensible. Only later did it occur to me that I should have been much more relieved that I would not be competing.

We went to the match, an away match, in matching glam outfits. I was acutely aware of my lack of underwear and that my padlock was off, both these things an omen of what would happen if our team lost. I was nervous of that, but not for long. My squad-mates attacked the match with relish and were easy 7-2 winners. They even took the ten cane strokes for the two events lost with good heart. For the first time since that first dreadful match six weeks ago, I had a pain-free Sunday. I spent much of the day rubbing healing cream into the wounds of my three team-mates. I could even bear to watch Match Of The day without cringing. Tibbet's Tits had also won and we remained two points (one win) behind them. I gathered that we weren't due to play them again this season and all we could do now was keep winning and hope they slip up.

On Monday we were back in training. I was very fit before arrival here and was catching up with the rest of the girls and I was really working on the other skills. In the afternoon we had the first karate session. There were several clubs in the city and Ian had been to one of them and got me a black belt which I wore with my bra and panties. The girls worked hard and enjoyed it, and so did I.

Tuesday, Wednesday and Thursday went by. I was really getting into the training. But on Friday the nervous tension returned as our training ceased ready for Saturday's match. For me the nerves were greater, because it was announced that this time I was in the team.

We were at home to a team just above the bottom two and it should be a comparatively easy win, so they were prepared to risk me, knowing the other girls could carry the match if need be. I wasn't having any of that, dears! I stripped off in front of the crowd with the usual gut-wrenching self-consciousness, but also with a touch of defiance. The events hurt and humiliated me, but I made sure that I was no passenger: in fact, several times, even with such warriors in my team, I led the way.

We won 9-0. We did not have to go into the stocks at all. I watched, bathed in sweat and covered in bruises, as the opposition girls screamed through the maximum ninety strokes of the cane. I was sorry for them, but not so sorry that I would want to take their place.

And after that performance, Sutton's Slags accepted me as one of them.

The season rolled on. The training was great, the matches horrible. We won every remaining match, but Tibbet's Tits had beaten us home and away and had lost only two other matches to our one (all before my arrival), so they took the league title. Mr. Sutton had long since accepted that this would be so: but he wanted and expected us to do better next season. So did we.

CHAPTER SEVEN
Narrator

The last match of the season was over.

Tibbet's Tits had won the league, for the third year running, but the common consensus was that Sutton's Slags had pushed them hard and emerged as serious contenders for next year. Nicky, recovering from that last match - an emphatic 8-1 win over a team in the lower half of the league, watched the analysis on Match Of The Day. Her relief that there would be no more of these dreadful Saturdays, at least for a while, was overpowering, so much so that the usual shame and embarrassment as she saw the image of her naked body on the screen was barely noticeable in comparision.

"I really think that the purchase of Nicky Nipples has been the last piece of the jigsaw for Sutton's Slags," one of the commentators was saying. "They haven't lost a match since she was added to the squad."

"Indeed," said a familiar voice from behind Nicky.

She turned round on the bed to see John Sutton, her owner, standing behind her. She hadn't heard him come in.

"No, don't get up," he said as she began to scramble to her feet, or rather her knees. "You played well again yesterday."

"Thank you, Master." Only five cane marks decorated Nicky's backside. Winning many of the other events, though, brought pains of their own.

"Now you get the reward of being an arena slave. You have three months' rest before we start pre-season training."

"Yes, master. Thank you, master." Oh, the relief!

"I expect you to keep fit, though. You'll be scheduled for three sessions in the gym per week. Apart from that, you'll be able to go out and about and enjoy the city, almost as if you were free."

"Yes, master." It was as good, if not better, than she could possibly have expected. She would have wanted to keep the gym up anyway: Nicky liked being fit, and she had never been fitter than she was now, although she did need a rest as well. It was still 'almost' as if she were free, but Nicky had resigned herself now to the fact that there was no escape from here. Only if they decided to let her go - very unlikely - would she ever be truly free again.

In the meantime, however, she had been nerving herself for one thing and this was a heaven-sent opportunity to bring it up.

"Master, permission to speak?"

"Very well."

"They said on the television that I was the last piece of the jigsaw for the squad, but I think there's somebody else who we could use as well."

"Another player?"

"Yes, master. Katie Kunt."

Sutton racked his brain, then located the image he wanted. "Ah yes, the lightweight girl in your team when you were with Thornton's Fillies. Hmm."

"She's very athletic and determined, at least when she has a chance. A season of being crowd-raped more weeks than not hasn't done her any favours, but when we were in matches together she was really good. Trouble was, Gemma Jism was okay but there were two other pretty useless girls in the team and they dragged us down. Put Katie in a strong team and I think she'd be a big asset." Nicky was trying to help rescue Katie from the nightmare of Thornton's Fillies, but she was also genuinely convinced that the lithe, elfin athlete could strengthen Sutton's Slags.

"She's very light, though."

"So play her only in home games and choose the optional events with that in mind."

Sutton reflected. "I'll watch some of the video footage and then make enquiries. I might buy her but not put her onto the squad straight away, see how she gets on in training."

Which was why, two weeks later, Katie arrived at the Sutton mansion. Thornton was quite happy to take the money and buy a fresh girl. Knowing that Nicky had recommended her, Katie went straight to the cherry-red beauty and kissed her warmly. No summer holiday for Katie, though: she was put straight away into training. Even so, it was a wonderful escape from Thornton.

Nicky took a deep breath of delightful sea air and adjusted her beach bag over her shoulder. Her feet felt the fine sand as her sandals sunk into it as she padded along the beach, seeking a quiet spot. There were plenty of sun-worshippers around, but it was a long and spacious beach, so finding somewhere quiet would not be difficult. Truthfully, however, she was not in too much of a hurry to be alone. Nicky was wearing a smart, expensive bikini which showed off her beautifully toned body to perfection and she was well aware of the admiring glances she was attracting from a lot of young men on the beach. She had been pleasantly surprised to find that she was enjoying this: before her kidnapping, she wouldn't have had the nerve for it. Now her greatest fear was of being recognised, but so far so good, and this was her third day on the beach.

She wasn't entirely free, of course: when all was said and done she was still a slave. However, as long as she told her handlers where she was going, her days were her own. She had no money, but in the mansion there were plenty of clothes and accessories she could borrow, all high quality, including this bikini. There was one other thing she was required to wear: but the little golden padlock between her legs fortunately did not show its outline through the bikini, nor did her nipple rings, so nobody could tell that she was a slave.

Nicky found a spot and settled down to soak up the sun. It was delicious. To her surprise, she even found herself considering removing her bikini top. She would never have done that back home. There were quite a few others around here going topless, but Nicky decided against it, not on the grounds of modesty but because her nipple rings would be a dead giveaway to her slave status. Some days she was recognised, some days not: in the close season for the league, the male public soon had other naked slaves to occupy their leering attention.

Sometime later, a handsome young man came over to her, introducing himself as Phil. As they got chatting, Nicky quietly admired his bronzed, muscular body and knew that he in turn was admiring her. It was nice. Minutes turned into an hour, then two. He bought her an ice cream (as a slave, she had no money, but she managed without actually lying to suggest that she had left her purse at home) and soon she found his arm around her bare shoulders and her arm around his. They went for a swim together (her padlock, still hidden beneath her bikini, was stainless steel) and eventually began kissing. He wasn't forcing the pace and she was quite comfortable, except that she was aware that he didn't know she was a slave: somehow she had just never got around to telling him. Well, did he have to know?

But as the day wore on and they became more comfortable and intimate with each other, Nicky realised where they were heading. She was still perfectly happy with that, except that she knew that it couldn't happen: beneath her bikini bottoms, the little padlock would bar all visitors to her inner person. There was nothing she could do about it. In fairness to Phil, she had to tell him, but she couldn't bring herself to do it until they were close to the edge. As they surfaced from a long French kiss and she felt his hand on her bra clip, Nicky said breathlessly, "Phil ... I can't!"

He immediately backed off. "I'm sorry, Nicky ... I thought ..."

She miserably felt barriers springing up between them. "No ... I want it as much as you; but I can't."

He looked puzzled. "Wrong time of the month?"

There was a perfect alibi, but Nicky forced herself to be honest. However, she couldn't bring herself to say it. Instead, she took his hand and guided it into her panties, down until her felt the padlock. Phil's brow furrowed. Without speaking, he gently went back to the clasp of Nicky's bra and undid it. Nicky felt a flush of shame as the cups fell away. It wasn't the exposure of her breasts, in fact she wanted him to be looking at them, but she knew that the centre of his attention were her nipple rings, which confirmed what the padlock had suggested.

"You're an arena slave," he said quietly.

Tears were beginning to roll down Nicky's cheeks. "Yes," she said sadly. "I'm sorry: I should have told you earlier. If you get in touch with my owner, I'm sure he'll give me a good beating for masquerading."

"Don't be silly. What difference does you being a slave make?"

"Well, you're free and I'm just ..."

"You're just gorgeous and a really nice person to be with."

Nicky shivered with pleasure at both compliments. However, although her tears had stemmed, she felt she had to persist. "It makes a difference because you can't do what you wanted to do."

"Do you think that's all I wanted?"

"No, but ..." Whatever else Nicky intended to say was almost literally swallowed up as he kissed her once more, long and deep. For a long time they canoodled. However, despite his words, Nicky could feel the sexual frustration in him. She too felt the frustration, but whilst there was nothing she could do about her own sexual heat, his was another matter.

She stood up and grabbed his hand. "Come on," she said firmly.

He allowed himself to be pulled along. "Where are we going?"

"Up into the sand dunes," she replied. "It's more private up there."

"But I thought ..."

"Don't think. Trust me."

Those people nearby who saw them going would not find it difficult to surmise their intentions: Nicky, her bra now discarded and Phil looked to be in quite a hurry. She led him to a deserted spot among the dunes and they kissed again passionately; then Phil found her hand slipping into his shorts, finding his manhood and stimulating it. Her very touch made it go rock hard and, if she hadn't pulled his shorts down, it would have been rather uncomfortable for him.

Nicky broke off their kiss and looked at him with an enigmatic expression. "I really hope you don't think that I make a habit of doing this," she said coyly, "but it's the only way."

"What do you meaahhhhh!" Phil's voice went husky as he felt her lips on his manhood. A moment later his penis was engulfed inside her mouth. He built quickly to a climax and came fiercely. Nicky kept him in her mouth, swallowing down his come in gulps to keep from choking on it.

A little while later they lay in each other's arms. Phil was very conscious of the fact that Nicky had made sure he'd had his pleasure even though she was prevented from fully taking her own. He had been able to bring her off by stimulation, but he knew that it wasn't the same as penetration. Still, it was all her chastity lock would allow.

"So which team are you with?" he asked.

"Sutton's Slags."

He thought for a moment. "Are you the one they broke the transfer record for a couple of months ago? Of course: Nicky, Nicky Nipples. Hey, I'm dating a superstar!"

Nicky blushed. "A reluctant superstar," she pointed out.

"Is it bad?"

"Very. But, I'll survive." She didn't want the conversation to get sombre.

"I've only ever seen a few television highlights of matches. I think you must be incredibly brave."

"We don't get much choice," Nicky pointed out. "What do you do for a living?"xxx

"Not much, to be honest: my dad's worth pots. I work for him."

"Will he be angry that you've been with a lowly slave?"

"Nah, we get on great. He'll be fine, especially since it's you. He says you're very good: he's a Thornton's fan and he was in the audience for all your matches with them. In fact ..." Phil's voice trailed off.

"What?" Nicky prompted.

"Oh, nothing, nothing."

"Come on, tell me." Then she worked it out for herself. "He was there when we lost a match, wasn't he? He was one of the ones who lined up and raped me afterwards, wasn't he?"

"I'm sorry," said Phil quietly. "Yes."

There was a long silence. "I suppose you hate me now," said Phil quietly.

"Of course not," Nicky said. "I'm not even sure I hate your dad. It's just ... it all takes a lot of getting used to. Dozens of men had me that day and the next week and I don't even know who they are. And I'm sorry that your dad has enjoyed me but I can't give myself to you."

"I thought you just did a while ago, or as good as."

Nicky's embarrassed giggle was cut short as his lips met hers once more.

When she got home that evening, Nicky felt better than at any time since her abduction. She and Phil had arranged to meet tomorrow on the beach again. He had insisted that this time he would not allow her to go down on him, especially after she had confessed that it was the first time she had ever done it without being forced to, but Nicky had another plan. She asked if she could see her owner.

"Why?" her handler asked.

Nicky decided to be honest. "I met a boy on the beach. I want to beg Mr. Sutton to leave my padlock off tomorrow." The handler shrugged. Nicky asked him, "what do you think his response will be?"

"He'll either say yes, or give you a caning. Still want to see him?"

Nicky swallowed hard. "Yes," she said bravely.

A while later she was ushered into his presence, naked, the little padlock pulling on her sex lips ever so slightly. He looked up from his newspaper and pre-empted her. Clearly her handler had briefed him. "So," he said, "you only met this boy today? A bit of a fast mover, aren't you?"

Nicky coloured deeply. Although she had learnt that honesty was usually the safest policy for a slave, she felt it best not to mention that she had already had oral sex with Phil. "I ... since I've been enslaved, I've found that I have to grab what little comfort I can before I lose it," she tried to explain, hoping also to get on his good side by emphasising her acceptance of her slavery. "And I suppose I've lost a lot of inhibitions since being in the arena." This was certainly very true: she now stood at attention before him, hands by her sides, not even tempted to hide her charms.

"Hmm. Well, that chastity lock isn't there just for show. It's not a fashion accessory."

Nicky's spirits sank. "No, Master."

"You're supposed to be resting and recharging your batteries for next season."

"Yes, Master. Sorry, Master." Would she get caned for asking?

He sighed. "You teenagers are all just raging hormones aren't you? Well, you've done well enough with the team so far. I'll let you go unlocked tomorrow and after that once a week during the holiday."

Nicky's face lit up. "Thank you, Master!"

"Subject, if you'll let me finish, to this boy being checked out to make sure he's of good stock and family. I presume you paused long enough to find out his name and address?"

"Yes, Master."

"Give it to your handler, he'll make the appropriate enquiries tonight and if I'm satisfied, you'll be unlocked in the morning and you can leave your lock at home all day. Mind, this is only with this one boy, understand?"

Just how loose did he think she was? "Yes, Master, thank you, Master.

He dismissed her with a wave. It was bizarre, Nicky reflected later: she was thanking him profusely and genuinely for letting her do what she should, at her age, have the right to decide about herself and in privacy; but that was the Corvalle way of things, at least for slaves and anyway she had endured the cringing embarrassment of it all and was now looking forwards to tomorrow even more. She was already planning it: she wouldn't tell Phil at first, she would lead him on and then unveil herself, unlocked and ready for his pleasure. And hers.

The weeks passed. Nicky enjoyed the holiday. Phil was great company. He listened, impressed, to the stories of her karate days and with sympathy to the story of her abduction and enslavement.

"There have been slaves here for as long as I can remember," he said. "I suppose I've grown up with the concept. I don't like to see them mistreated, though."

"But the mere fact of them - us - being slaves is mistreatment," Nicky argued.

"Maybe. Like I said, I've grown up with it."

"Have you ever had sex with a slave?"

"Yes: with you!"

"Come on: you know what I mean."

"Of course I have, like every other man in this city. Quite a few times, actually. And no, I don't regret it. If I hadn't, someone else would have done."

"That's a cop out."

"I know, but it's the best I can do."

"You'll do better than that tomorrow," teased Nicky; "it's my day without my padlock!"

It was all too easy, at times, for Nicky to forget that she was a slave. Reality, however, has a way of intruding.

The next day, she and Phil were wandering down a quiet sea front on the far side of the city's long shoreline. Nicky was wearing a fetching but brief bikini. It was her weekly day when she was allowed out without her chastity padlock and she and Phil were intending to celebrate that, for a change, in the near-deserted woods outside this north end of the city.

As they kissed, both became aware of a young man, no more than eighteen years old, sitting with his parents on a bench watching them.

"I'm sure that's Nicky Nipples," the young man told his elders, not realising how his voice carried. "She's the one Sutton's Slags paid forty thousand pounds on the transfer market for."

"Don't see how any slave girl can be worth that much," his mother observed slightly huffily.

"Oh, I don't know," said the father. "John Sutton wants to win the league and with this girl added to his team he's got a real chance of that this season."

"Will you take me with you to see some matches this season, dad?" the youngster asked.

"Well, you're old enough now," said his father indulgently. "I don't see why not."

Nicky, pretending not to hear, shivered slightly. If her team lost when they came, father and son would both be in the queue for her. But then, so would many others. She and Phil moved on.

However, a quartet of young men had also recognised her. They followed for a little while, then stepped in front of the pair. Ignoring Phil, one said cheerfully, "hi, Nicky Nipples!"

She didn't know any of them. "Hello sir," she said cautiously.

"We're all fans of yours," the young man said, indicating his companions, all around Nicky's own age. "Show us your tits."

Nicky sighed. It was an order. Beside her, Phil tensed impotently, but in public these youths had as much right to her as he did. What Nicky herself wanted was unfortunately totally irrelevant.

Nicky pulled the bikini top over her head to reveal her boobs. As usual in such situations, her face went red, but it had to be done. If these kids complained to Mr. Sutton, it would be considered that he had a moral obligation to chastise her - and John Sutton took his civic responsibilities seriously. He had also spoken to the girls about the need to keep what he called a good public image and Nicky being reported for slave disobedience would not please him to say the least. It would likely lead to a hefty punishment and the loss of those little privileges such as being allowed out with Phil and even without her padlock, that made life bearable. She might even be placed on the transfer list! No: better to let these brats have their fun.

"I love to see you in the arena with lots of weights hanging from those rings," another of the youths leered.

"Yes, sir," was all Nicky could say. Perhaps, if he knew how much that hurt, to have several kilos stretching your nipples, he might see that differently. Or perhaps not.

"Well don't stop the stripping there," said another.

Glumly, Nicky lowered her bikini pants. She was suddenly very conscious that she did not have her padlock on. The lads saw that too.

"Hey, how about that, it's open season!" said a third.

"Hold on a moment," intruded Phil. "If an owner sends his slave out naked and unlocked, then by convention and tradition he's inviting you to have her. This girl was dressed."

The lads glowered at him. They knew he was correct and it was not what they wanted to hear. They hesitated. Tearaways or not, in this land it was good sense to obey the law. Breaking it could lead to some very unpleasant sentences, including a short sharp shock of enslavement of themselves.

"We can still have a good grope, though," countered the leader after a few moments. Phil was powerless to argue with that and had to watch as Nicky was pulled into the group of youths. She felt hands everywhere on her body and soon also lips and tongues. Nicky was mauled, French-kissed and spanked for long minutes. Passers-by made no comment and Phil could only watch helplessly. Eventually the youths tired of their sport and wandered off. However, they kept Nicky's bikini, despite Phil's protests.

"We're only borrowing it, the leader called back cheerfully. "We'll drop it off at Sutton's place later."

Unable to dissuade them and relieved to see them go, Phil turned to Nicky. She was stood, hands covering up her breasts, her now fully re-grown pubic hair fully on show. She was shaking. Phil knew she had endured worse in the arena, but realised that this had been sudden and unexpected and also a very forceful reminder of her status and lack of rights or security in this city. He put an arm gently around her and drew her to him.

"Fuck me," she whispered.

"Huh?"

"I'm only fuckmeat," she said, repeating how one of the young thugs had described her, "so fuck me! Please! There's no law against copulating with a slave in public, so do it! I'm begging you!"

He had to admit his own passion was inflamed by her nudity. They almost fell off the concourse onto the beach and did it there and then, a torrid riot of steaming passion. Later, they joined a second time, less urgently and more lovingly.

Later still, as she nestled in his arms, Phil said, "how are we going to get you home without clothes?"

"I'm a slave," Nicky said dully. "I'll walk."

"You go walking starkers through the streets without your padlock and you'll be had half a dozen times before you get home. I could nip back to my place and get you something to wear."

She shook her head. "If you leave me, they'll come back and they'll say that since I'm nude, they can have me. They can't if you're a witness." Nicky, as property, could not be a witness herself.

"Think that's why they did it?"

"Maybe; or maybe they were just being cruel." Nicky, these days, understood cruelty very well.

There was nothing else Phil could do. He hadn't brought any money or credit cards with him, nor a phone; he himself only wore shorts. He couldn't even give her those, because there was no law against indecent exposure for her as a slave, but there was for him. Anyway, Nicky wouldn't hear it. Bravely, she walked home naked. They tried to use the back streets and deserted passages as much as they could, or else conversely the busiest streets, where she might be seen but was unlikely to be rogered in quite such a public place.

They nearly made it. Unfortunately they met a lone man on one of the last streets who took one look at Nicky's nude, be-ringed body and commanded her to lie down on the grass verge and spread her legs. Nicky obeyed without fuss and Phil watched, dismayed, as this man had his way with her. He wiped his prick on her hair and departed without a word. Nicky said nothing, but snuggled up closer to Phil for the rest of the journey home. She found her bikini hanging on the gatepost of the bog house.

Nicky made no complaint or report of the whole incident to her owner or handler. There was no point. For a slave, it was an occupational hazard. It would not stop her going out during the summer.

But the dreaded start of the next league season grew closer. Pre-season training was only a week or so away. The league was getting more competitive, with only a couple of teams (or rather owners) like Thornton not bothering about the results. Sutton's Slags would have three weeks' intensive fitness and endurance training before the awful matches started. Nicky's period of freedom was nearing its end.

And one night, as she returned from another delightful day with Phil, she was summoned.

"Mr. Sutton wants to see you," Katie whispered. "It sounds like trouble."

Nicky frantically wondered what she had done wrong. She had good reason to be scared: if her owner decided she should be punished, she had no say or appeal in the matter: he was judge, jury and executioner. She stood nervously to attention in his lounge, stark naked, her padlock polished and gleaming as it hung between her now well-tanned legs.

He kept her waiting while he sorted some paperwork: she was only a slave, after all. Eventually he looked up.

"You've been seeing this young lad all summer, haven't you?"

"Y-yes, Master. I didn't think I wasn't supposed to."

"I didn't say you weren't. But did you know that his father has put in a bid to buy you?"

Nicky's jaw dropped open. "N-no," she stammered, taken aback.

"He offered quite a good price, actually, a fair bit more than I paid for you."

"I didn't know anything about it," Nicky protested honestly.

"Good. I wouldn't like to think that you were not committed to our dream of winning the league this season."

Nicky took a deep breath. "I'm committed," she said with conviction. League matches meant atrocious pain, dreadful humiliation and unwanted intimacy, invasion of her privacy and of her body and the total shredding of her dignity; but she meant it about being committed. If she had to be in the league, she wanted to win it. It wasn't just the avoidance of the crowd rape - it was inevitable that they couldn't possibly win every game - and the cane, or another public shaving of her mound. Nicky's fierce competitive instinct had taken over. Although it meant humiliation and pain, the debasement of her body and embarrassment beyond measure, she would win.

"Well," Sutton said, "you'll be pleased to know that I have no intention of selling you." There had, to be truthful, been a flicker of hope in Nicky's heart that she would be spared the coming season. It died abruptly. "So I don't want you distracted by a boyfriend."

"No, Master." More than any father or coach, he had the power to ensure that, as the golden padlock between her legs testified.

"But as long as your performances are superb, you will be allowed to see this lad once a week. Only for an hour or so, mind, and with your chastity lock on."

Nicky brightened. She had been anticipating a complete ban and this was a bonus she hadn't expected. "Thank you, Master!"

"Only if your performances are absolutely top notch, remember."

"They will be, master. I am looking forward to getting into training."

"And the matches?"

Nicky grimaced. "I'll endure them, Master." It was impossible that anyone could look forward to competing in the arena.

The next day, Nicky was quick to bring up the subject of the offer to buy her with Phil.

"Yes, dad wanted to buy you for me," he admitted.

"Would you have freed me?"

"Hell, no. Dad's an altruist up to a point, but the price he had to offer for you was pretty steep. We could buy half a dozen common girls in the market for that."

"I suppose I should be flattered."

"But you'd have had a much easier time with me than in the arena."

Nicky knew that, but the whole thing was reinforcing the point that there was still no way out of slavery altogether for her. As it turned out, there was no way out of the arena either. "Mr. Sutton didn't want to sell me."

"Not at any realistic price. I'm afraid you're stuck with another season in the league."

Nicky nodded soberly. "Thanks for trying." She thought for a moment, then tentatively asked: "if - just if - your dad was to offer a whole lot more money for me, enough that even Sutton wouldn't say no and bought me and then freed me; if I could get back to England, I could repay him and more."

Phil shook his head. "As a slave, we'd never get an export licence for you; and freed slaves are not allowed to leave the city."

"Oh." It had been worth a try.

Phil changed the subject. "Should I come to matches this season to support you?"

"No," Nicky answered decisively. "The things I have to do in the arena are unbearably humiliating. I wouldn't want you to see me like that. But thanks for the offer."

Later, however, she changed her mind and took Phil up on his offer. Nicky wasn't really sure why. Perhaps she just felt as if she wanted some support, although in fairness the Sutton fans did support the girls, for all that they enjoyed the pain of the spectacle. Or perhaps it was that, at the end of the day, she WAS an arena slave and had to accept it.

CHAPTER EIGHT
Narrator

Nicky had always been very fit, but the training with Sutton's Slags towards the end of last season had honed that fitness still sharper and during the close season regular gym sessions had kept her standard up. Now two weeks of intensive pre-season training and good diet, without the interruption of matches, brought her to a peak of fitness beyond anything she had ever known. The rest of her squad, too, were brimming with energy.

Katie was training with the squad, but had not been registered as a squad member. The league rules allowed only five girls in a squad and Mr. Sutton felt it best for the moment to stick with the team he had. Katie was competitive, athletic and determined, but so were the rest of his girls and her slightness of stature, at just 48 kilos, might tell against her. However, she was being kept as a reserve, in the peak of readiness, in case of an injury or illness to one of the regulars, or if things started to go badly in the league and Mr. Sutton felt the need to freshen the team and change tactics with home matches.

Katie was generally kept naked, as a result of which it was plain to all that her fine pussy hair had grown back fully now. Her rings had been kept in, but, as she was not actually on the squad, her padlock had been removed. She was used from time to time by the male house staff and handlers for sex which, having no choice in the matter, she put a brave face on, and in addition to training, she had domestic duties, including waiting on the five girls in the squad. Nicky didn't want this at first, but Katie herself insisted: she was extremely grateful to Nicky for rescuing her from the hell of being a Thornton Filly. Life here was so much better and of course she did not have to go into the arena. However, Katie confessed to Nicky that she was actually missing the competitiveness of it all and was determined to train hard ready for when her chance to get on this great team came. Nicky found this attitude surprising. And yet ...

Tension rose as the opening day of the season neared. Nicky was actually relieved to be selected for the team in the first match: at least it would get it over with. She stripped nude in the arena, feeling her usual cringing embarrassment and yet buoyed just a little by the cheering of the Sutton fans.

Nicky's team braved substantial pain to put down an 8-1 win as a marker for the season against a good mid-table side. Tibbet's Tits won 6-3 and so Sutton's Slags topped the table on event difference - the equivalent of goal difference in football. The next week, against a (comparatively) easy team, they clocked up a 9-0 victory, and, with Nicky rested the week after that, a 6-3 win kept them top of the table. The Tits also had three wins out of three and one other team was also on maximum wins, so the league table was taking shape.

Nicky realised that during matches she was no longer trying her best because of the cane, or the penalty of crowd rape. She wanted to win. They all did. The team was changed each week by rotation, adjusting to take account of opposition (both strength and likely option event choices), and the two girls left out were actually less happy than the three picked for the match. Nicky also realised with a shock that she did not want to lose her place on the squad to Katie. None of the other girls did either. With an astuteness that impressed Nicky, their trainer and their owner took Katie off domestic duties and had her training with the squad more or less full time, also restricting sexual access to Katie to just the two of them and the two handlers; and with two other domestic slave girls available, that kept Katie's entertainment duties quite light. The pressure on the squad to win was being cranked up; and they responded in kind. They won match after match. The Tits were also winning, but by slightly lower margins, so the Slags stayed top of the league. However, they all knew that so much would depend on the home and away matches between the two teams. They were scheduled to play at the Tits' arena, the so-called Theatre Of Anguish, in a few weeks' time and then the return at Slag Stadium on the last day of the season - a cliff-hanger if ever there was.

Interest in the league was massive, especially with this tight battle for the championship. Several of the teams immediately below the top two were openly talking about development plans to challenge for the title next year, if not this. The league was to be expanded from twelve to fourteen teams next year, to the consternation of the arena girls, who would now face an extra four matches per year; but of course they had no say in the matter. Nicky found that she was being recognised almost whenever she stepped outside Slagland, the Sutton mansion: her chastity padlock was now an essential item for her own protection, although the team's trainer had banned her from sex with Phil anyway to keep her focused. However, most of the attention she got from passers-by was actually adulation: she was even being asked for her autograph. At first she would sign it just 'Nicky', but after a while it became 'Nicky Nipples'. It simply did not occur to her to sign it 'Nicky Downing'.

Commercial opportunities, which the Tits had dominated for a long time, were increasing for all the league teams, but particularly the Slags. Mr. Sutton was cautious about anything which might deflect their attention from training, but on the advice of Ian, their trainer, began to use Fridays for this to ease some of the debilitating pre-match tension; and also some Wednesday afternoons were used to break up the training monotony. Thus it was that Nicky found herself at a car show one Friday, spending all day draped over a car bonnet in a minuscule bikini and actually thoroughly enjoying every moment of it.

Another Wednesday afternoon was spent modelling clothes on a catwalk, which did her self-confidence a power of good. Now she thought about her old rival, Claire Sanderson, again. Claire had dabbled a bit in modelling, using contacts from her well-placed family to do a couple of very minor shoots, but nothing as major as this.

The next week's shoot, however, brought Nicky down to earth a little bit: it was a beach job for sun tan lotion and would again have been great fun except for the fact that she was ordered to do it stark naked. Nicky just had to put on the bravest face she could. After all, she had to strip most weekends in the arena, except when she wasn't in the team, and nude colour pictures from matches had appeared in the local newspaper, sometimes in extremely unflattering situations during the events. Worse still was when she and the other Slags were made to do a series of full frontal shots for pin-up posters, which became big sellers. A lot of youths and much older men for that matter, soon had full length posters of Nicky on their bedroom walls to masturbate to at night. Sometimes that thought made her cringe, other times she just glumly accepted it. It was also not nice to be walking down the street and see a huge poster of yourself, showing everything you have, on an adshell or the side of a building.

The amount of money these promotions were earning was considerable: at least that was one in the eye for Claire Sanderson: Nicky had earned more in one afternoon than Claire could have done in a month. Of course, the money did not go to her, but to her owner: Nicky, by law, could not actually own money or anything else for that matter - even her treasured karate medal belonged to her owner. However, in another astute move, Mr. Sutton had announced that half of the money the girls were earning would go to charity; and he also let the girls themselves choose the actual causes. That was a particularly enjoyable task for Nicky: the old people's hospice in her home town would never know where the carefully anonymously donated money came from, but that didn't matter. She even approached her next nude shoot with a bit less reluctance.

It was also becoming clear that Nicky was emerging as one of the brightest stars of the team. She was not the team captain, but her efforts in the arena were second to none. There was no rivalry between the girls, though: each of them gave their utmost, in both training and the arena. Katie was fully accepted by the others, even though officially not part of the team; and she too attracted a bit of media attention. She was still elfin, but her fitness and athleticism were outstanding and she was raring to go. Most commentators opined that she would be brought in at some point during the second half of the season to freshen the team. Incredibly, not one of the current squad wanted to lose their place to her, even though it would mean them escaping those dreadful, pain and humiliation-filled Saturdays in the arena. Their camaraderie was that intense.

That feeling even affected their owner. John Sutton ensured that in the evenings they wanted for nothing. It might be a gilded cage, but Nicky's room and their social area contained luxuries she would not have dreamt of at home. Their trainer, Ian, oozed respect for them, which did not make him ease off on their training one slightest bit, nor would they have it any other way: his strap still stung - and often. John Sutton even forsake his Mercedes and rode in their people carrier with them to matches. On the way to one game, he turned to them and said thoughtfully, "you know, slaves, I've been wondering whether your team name is a bit harsh these days. Maybe Sutton's Slags should change their name to Sutton's Superheroines, or Supermodels, or something like that."

There was quiet for a few moments as the girls digested this. It was obvious that he was paying them a considerable compliment. Then one girl responded quietly but with feeling, "I'm a Slag, Master."

Nicky spoke up. "I'm a Sutton's Slag, Master," she affirmed vehemently. As the other girls agreed one by one, Nicky reflected with some incredulity on what she had just said. Even her use of the word 'Master' had been said with total acceptance, even pride. Then Katie piped up, last of all: "I want to be a Sutton's Slag, master!" Everyone collapsed into laughter and Katie was hugged by each of the girls in turn.

John Sutton grinned and said, "see me in my room tonight, mini-Slag!"

"Yes, master," Katie replied chirpily. Everybody knew how Katie would now be spending the evening and the once innocent eighteen year-old blushed only slightly.

It would be another full house today. Each match of the Slags and the Tits was sold out, to the consternation of the opposing teams, because it meant huge queues of men for the crowd-rape afterwards; and if you were up against the Slags or the Tits, chances were you would be on the losing team and in the rape racks afterwards. Teams tried their best, often raising the pain level for both sides substantially; but still the Slags and the Tits went marching on towards their first cataclysmic confrontation with each other this season, for which even the Theatre Of Anguish was sold out within a day of the tickets going on sale.

Nicky stood, naked, with two of her team-mates. Absolute exhaustion made it difficult for them to stay on their feet and their incredibly battered bodies were black and blue all over. But the worst agony was in their hearts.

The arena scoreboard read: Tibbet's Tits 5, Sutton's Slags 4.

They had tried. It was the strongest team they could put out and they had endured incredible torment with grim, unfaltering determination. They had put themselves through Hell. But they had still lost. They won the compulsory events 3-2, but had lost three of the four optional ones. Clearly the Tits had been training for weeks on just these four particular activities, inuring themselves, numbing their bodies, whilst the Slags had only found out what the events were while actually in the arena. For weeks they, too, had tried to cover each possibility: but the list of allowed options was too long, too wide to cover everything comprehensively enough.

Wordlessly, the other two girls in the squad came over to them and slipped off their glamour dresses ready for the ordeal that was to come. There were six hundred men in the audience, every seat filled and then some. Two thirds of them were Tibbet fans and not one was likely to want to miss this chance to thoroughly screw their team's rivals.

As for the Sutton fans, this was the first chance all season to taste the girls that they loved and supported.

Out of the corner of her eye, Nicky saw Katie whispering to John Sutton in the front seats at the arena edge. Then she saw Sutton's hand delve under Katie's short skirt. Her numb mind vaguely puzzled over this, because it seemed very unlikely that either of them felt like sex right now; but then Sutton's hand came out again, holding Katie's padlock and the elfin teenager ducked under the barrier, pulled her dress off and ran naked over to her comrades. Somehow the rape racks would have to accommodate six girls rather than five. This was not a ploy to get Katie into the team and certainly not something she would enjoy: she just wanted to stand by her friends in their darkest hour. And six hundred divided by six was marginally less awful than six hundred divided by five.

It was finally brought home who was the biggest star of the team when Nicky was selected for the shaving. Every inch of her body on fire with pain, she staggered up to the chair and whimpered as the leg holsters were pulled wide. Staring at the arena ceiling with tears running down her eyes, Nicky felt the shaving foam being daubed on her triangle and a razor scraping the hair away until her skin was baby-smooth. Her baldness now a very visible badge of shame, she rejoined her two match colleagues - Katie and the other two were already secured in the rape racks, writhing under the first of many men - and they staggered towards the stocks. They would get fifty strokes; Nicky had not had more than fifteen all season so far. Well, they deserved it, even if it was on bottoms already swollen up like balloons; and beyond that, hundreds of men were quietly massaging their pricks, ready to drive them into the tender bodies of Nicky and her friends.

Nicky cried out in pain as the cane was just gently placed on her heavily wealed bottom, the caner measuring his swing. When the first stroke sliced through the weals and into her flesh, she screamed.

There is a limit to have much flesh and blood can stand

Nicky and the other two girls in the match team spent the next three days in hospital recovering; Katie and the two reserves, after the crowd rape, were kept in overnight on Saturday evening, or rather from Sunday morning, as the queues did not dissipate until the early hours. Numerous buckets of water had had to be thrown over the girls, particularly the three match team girls, to keep them conscious through the long hours of their rape ordeal.

Although they were thoroughly pampered in the hospital - several of the nurses and doctors were fans - Nicky was not allowed to forget that she was a slave. Late on Sunday afternoon, a newspaper photographer came and photographed her, full frontal, all of her bandages removed so that her welts and weals and bruises could all be seen. She also had to roll over so that her purple, heavily swollen bottom could be captured on film. Nicky accepted the invasion of what ought to have been her privacy without the slightest qualm: her master ordered, so it was done. Her own discomfort or embarrassment simply had to be borne. She was a true slave now, totally accepting John Sutton's ownership of her, his absolute right to do with her as he wished. Even if he sold her, she would accept it and transfer her obedience to her new owner; but she could only pray that that would not happen, because she was totally committed to winning the league.

The match received huge publicity, even more than the pre-match hype. The photographs of Nicky and the other girls' cruelly battered bodies might have put people off had it not been for the heartfelt quotes from them that they would be back in the arena as soon as they were allowed. The local newspaper brought out a special edition with massive colour pictures, proclaiming it the battle of the century, round one. The Tits, of course, had to come to Slag Stadium for the rematch on the last day of the season. With home advantage (from being able to choose the option events), the Slags could well turn things around and, if they kept their superior event difference, win the league.

Katie was brought into the squad. There was no alternative, really: neither Nicky nor the other two who fought the match would be able to return to action for the game the following Saturday. Sadie, the girl Katie replaced, was inconsolable. John Sutton himself both broke the news and comforted her. She was to remain training with the squad and would take Katie's place as the sexual relief of Ian the trainer, Sutton himself and the other mansion staff; and she was to consider herself still a vital part of the team.

The girls were no longer required to wear their chastity padlocks within the mansion and training centre. The five players in the squad were simply ordered to remain celibate and trusted to obey that order. Proud of being trusted, Nicky had not the slightest intention of disobeying any order, but also would not do anything that might affect her performance and her pent-up emotions did help the number of times she could orgasm on the second event each week. Only when leaving the mansion for any reason, except to compete in a match, were the girls locked, and even then only to prevent them being molested against their will. Nicky was locked for her weekly dates with Phil, but sometimes he was now allowed to visit the mansion and she was allowed to be alone with him unlocked, as he was trusted not to force himself on her. He was actually offered Sadie as recompense and to Nicky's chagrin he accepted the offer; so when her (now extended) time allowed with him was up, she took him to Sadie's room and left him there, knowing he would be shagging her friend within minutes. But then, she was not in love with Phil, or he with her: it had just been a holiday fling which had moved into something akin to friendship until such time as Nicky was sexually free once more.

Katie made her debut the next Saturday in the home match, alongside the other two girls who had not been in the team the previous weekend. Nicky, still quite stiff and sore, was fully aware that if what was really the reserve team (the strongest three having been fielded against the Tits) lost, she would be crowd raped again, but she had faith in her friends. Her judgement was sound, because they won 6-3. The Tits, with two fresh players having to carry a still under par third (and they hadn't had the caning or crowd rape afterwards!) scraped home 5-4 in their match. Life returned to what passed in this bizarre world for normal.

Another thing which resumed was the Sutton karate club. Nicky's lessons to the other girls had developed into a full club, run two evenings a week. The girls were keen and Ian the trainer had approved it. Mr. Sutton had bought them kits, punch bags and whatever other equipment Nicky had asked for. With such fit, focused girls and their bond with Nicky, they had quickly developed into a good group. A rare weekend off during the league season was coming up, with no matches because of some other event in the city. On the Sunday, the main karate club in the city was holding a big open tournament. Nicky got permission from Mr. Sutton for her girls to compete in the low grades section, whilst she would take part in the black belts event. It would be hard work for her girls, but much less demanding or painful than a league match!

And so it was, as she led her team into the booking-in, that she bumped into her old karate coach, Vic, and her former bitter rival, Claire Sanderson.

CHAPTER NINE
Narrator

There was a long, stunned silence. Then Nicky and Vic hugged each other in a rare and fierce show of emotion.

Confusion reigned for a few moments. Then, leaving her girls with Ian to get booked in, they moved to somewhere quieter.

"We all thought you were dead," said Vic, as if in a dream. "I went to your funeral. I cried buckets."

Nicky was wondering just how she was going to explain all this. Her first thought was if it would affect her in the league. Only later did it begin to occur to her that this could be her ticket out of here.

"I was abducted and brought here," she said and then hesitated. How to explain what she was now to this man she respected so much? She changed the subject, to stall for time. "How about you? What are you doing now?"

A shadow crossed Vic's mouth. "When I thought you had ... gone, I was inconsolable. After a while, Claire asked me to be her personal coach. I know you two didn't get on, and she isn't a patch on you either as a person or a player, but ..."

"I don't mind," Nicky said truthfully. "You're too good a coach to waste on just club players."

Vic looked relieved. "Well, Claire's family is rolling in money, so she could afford to go to tournaments all over and take me with her. She found this one on an obscure site on the internet and, as we had a major event in Argentina last week, she thought we'd pop over the mountains and do this one as well. We had a devil of a job getting visas, though. We got in after being absolutely sworn to secrecy on the bizarre things that apparently go on here." He looked at her shrewdly. "You're mixed up in all that, I presume?"

"Up to my eyeballs," Nicky said wryly. Vic waited patiently. "I was sold as a slave," she said eventually.

His look of sympathy would have melted many a hard heart. "Are you still ..."

"Yes," she said shortly.

"I'm so sorry."

She shrugged. "It doesn't matter now, it's happened and that's it. I only ..." she looked him in the eye. "Vic, I want you to know that I didn't let you down. I submitted because I had to, but they said I was brave in the way I took it all. You taught me to be brave and I didn't forget it."

He put an arm around her. "You never let me down, ever," he said softly. "I'm just so glad you're alive."

"So am I," she said, suddenly very positive. "Vic, I'm an arena slave."

He winced. "I've heard just a bit about this league of theirs and the arenas. From what I've heard, it's very tough."

Nicky smiled. "You taught me how to be strong and tough."

"You always were a fighter and a survivor," he said admiringly. "So, how are we going to get you out of this?"

A shadow crossed Nicky's pretty face. "I don't think you can. They won't let me go. If you cause a fuss, they might not let you go either." Despite everything, a wicked smile came across her face. "Maybe they'd make Claire a slave too."

"Now, now," he chided very gently.

"In any case ..." Nicky felt herself on the edge of a precipice. She took a breath and fell over the cusp. "I can't leave before the end of the season. My team and I have the chance to win the league." What she was saying sounded incredible even to her own ears. Then she made another astonishing decision. "I'd like you to come and see me in a match," she said.

"Are you sure? I gather that matches are a bit ..."

"Yes, I'm sure," she said firmly. "Next Saturday: can you stay that long?"

"We weren't planning to, but of course; if it's what you really want."

"It is. I'll ask my owner if he could put you up at the mansion: there's space for visitors. Meanwhile," she said, her equilibrium restored, "I've got to get booked in for this karate competition. See what you think of my pupils."

Her pupils did well and Vic was thoroughly impressed. Nicky herself showed she had lost none of her old prowess. She cruised into the final, where she met Claire. Nicky had always had the edge between the two of them and although she hadn't trained properly for the best part of a year now, her fitness and strength were way above her old, already high levels. She blew Claire away to take the gold.

Changed back some time later, after the medals ceremony, into her brand new club tracksuit provided by Mr. Sutton - the girls had unanimously decided to call themselves Sutton's Slags - Nicky was waiting for the reception being given for all competitors when a steward stopped her. "Nicky Nipples?" he asked.

"Yes sir," Nicky affirmed, immediately dropping into the now instinctive slave mode.

"Come with me, please." Nicky followed him with some concern, but in the absence of either her owner or her trainer as his representative, she was obliged to obey the order of a free person. Ian, after putting her padlock back on when she changed, had gone ahead to get ready for the reception.

The steward led her into a room in the residential section of the leisure complex and, after ushering her inside, closed the door.

"Hello Nicky," said Claire Sanderson.

"Hello Claire," said Nicky warily.

"Tut, tut, tut," reproved Claire gently. "Now I did quite a bit of research on the ways of Corvalle before we came here. For one thing, I happen to know that is not the correct way for a slave to address a free person, is it?"

Nicky coloured. "No, miss," she said quietly. She had no choice but to go along with this.

"That's better," said Claire easily. "You see, I was quite intrigued when I stumbled onto this slave system in this city. I found just a hint of it when I discovered the entry form for the competition: there was a clause in the small print which said slaves were allowed to compete on level terms with free people. I read that and then I just kept digging. Unknown to poor Vic, I wanted to come and see what it was like; thought there might be some fun to be had. I never dreamed I would find you here. What luck!

"Now," she went on, "you might remember that back home I'm pretty good at winding the boys round my little finger, including the one you tried to entice away from me ..."

"I never ..." Nicky began, and then stopped herself.

Claire ignored her and carried on. "But I thought, what fun to actually have a real slave boy to attend to my needs. I don't like upsetting poor Vic, though, so I keep him discreetly in the cupboard." She walked over to a wall and slid a panel back. Stood amongst the clothes on hangars was a wickedly attractive, bronzed young Spanish man of around Nicky and Claire's age. "Come out, Pedro," Claire said playfully.

The young slave stepped out of the closet. He was superbly muscular and wore only a thong which bulged considerably with what must be an impressive manhood. His bare, muscular buttocks rippled as he moved.

Claire settled into an easy chair. "There's a company here which hires these boys out," she explained. "Do you like him?"

"He's ... very handsome, miss," said Nicky. The Spaniard seemed to almost smoulder.

"He's used to having to entertain middle aged viragos, so I reckon he's quite pleased that I picked him," Claire said. Nicky did not reply, but silently she tended to agree: for all her character faults, Claire was an extremely pretty blonde with a very good figure. "Is that right, Pedro?" Claire asked.

"Yes, miss," said the Spanish lad in fluent English. Even his voice was undeniably sexy, almost a husky growl.

Claire sat down in an easy chair. "Champagne," she ordered to Pedro, who padded off to the fridge in the adjoining room. Both girls watched those rippling muscles in his buttocks as he moved. He returned with a chilled glass of sparkling liquid from which Claire sipped leisurely. Nicky wondered where all this was leading.

"Anyway," Claire said, obviously enjoying herself immensely, "I paid good money for Pedro, but I have to say he's been worth it. He's superb in bed, Nicky, really fantastic. So, when I saw you today I thought, I know Pedro enjoys servicing me, but let's give him a bonus: you. At the same time, you must have to go with some pretty repulsive men, so I thought you'd like a nice change."

She sipped her drink again, then said: "I'm going to let the two of you screw each other."

Pedro's face was impassive, but his eyes shone greedily. Nicky went hot and cold. "I ... can't, miss," she said.

"Oh? And why not?"

Nicky coloured deeply. "I ... have to have permission from my owner to have sex."

"Well, we'll see about that. Why don't you take your clothes off, show him what he might be getting?"

She might just as well have barked out the word 'strip!' at the top of her voice. Nicky had no option. She pushed her trainers off with her heels and then unzipped her tracksuit top and pulled it off. Then she pulled her white t-shirt off to reveal her breasts and be-ringed nipples. She never liked stripping, but it was quite a while since she had been this embarrassed by it. Still, worse was yet to come. She pushed her tracksuit bottoms down her legs and stepped out of them, then pushed the white panties down. The little golden padlock swung free between her legs, stretching her labia slightly. Her pubic hair had still not fully grown back from her recent shaving after the defeat against the Tits, but there was now a covering of short, dark hairs on her mound. Nicky stood, incongruously still wearing white ankle socks, her hands clenched by her sides.

"You've added a couple of accessories since I last saw you in the showers a year or so ago," Claire observed, looking at Nicky's rings and the humiliating padlock.

"Yes miss," Nicky managed.

"What do you think, Pedro?" Claire asked the young man. "Could you make some nice music with that body?"

"Yes miss," said Pedro, staring at Nicky. "She's gorgeous!"

"Not as good as me, though," Claire prompted, slightly nettled.

"No, miss, that goes without saying," Pedro recovered smoothly.

"Why don't you have a feel of those hooters, Pedro?" Claire suggested. "Invite him, Nicky, you know you want to."

"W-why don't you have a feel of my boobs, Pedro?" Nicky invited, cringing with shame.

Pedro moved over and his strong hands closed over Nicky's melons, squeezing them roughly. "Very nice and firm, miss," he reported to Claire.

"I'm sure she'll soon invite you to check the rest of her hot little body, too," Claire said.

"You - you can put your hands anywhere you want," Nicky stammered and raised her hands away from her body. Momentarily Pedro's hands were all over her, caressing and feeling. Nicky shuddered: he was very sexy.

"Nice, Pedro?" Claire asked.

"Yes, miss: not as good as you, of course, but still pretty nice."

"A constant diet of caviar can leave you a bit jaded," Claire said. "A bit of pork pie makes a nice change."

"Exactly, miss."

"Talking of pork pie," Claire went on, "it's a shame about that padlock, isn't it Nicky?"

"Y-yes, miss." Pedro was pretty hunky, it was true; but Nicky was still extremely grateful that she wouldn't have to be screwed in front of her old, bitter rival.

"Well, that's easily solved," smiled Claire. "After our final, I had a brief word with your Mr. Sutton: told him how we were such good friends of old and how much I knew you would like sharing a bit of Pedro with me, just so I could show there were no hard feelings about you beating me in the final. He said that since there's six days before your next match, he could stretch a point." She dipped into her purse and pulled out a tiny key. With a sinking heart, Nicky recognised the key to her chastity lock. Claire pulled Pedro off her and Nicky heard the slight click of the key in the lock, felt the small weight lifted from her labia as the lock was removed. She glanced down at Pedro's pouch and saw that the bulge was considerably bigger now. He was all man, no doubt about that: but to be taken in front of Claire!

But Claire hadn't finished twisting the knife yet. "Now, before we move on to relieving Pedro's head of steam, there are a couple of things that must be straightened: a couple of errors on your part. I believe that when you first came into the room, you addressed me as 'Claire' rather than 'miss'. Correct?"

"Yes, miss." It could not be denied.

"You also, at one point early on, began to interrupt me?"

"Yes, miss."

"Well, as we're old friends, rather than reporting you, which I know I should, I'll deal with the matter myself. Do you think a good hand spanking would fit the bill?"

Oh God, how galling! "Yes, miss."

"I'm doing you a big favour, keeping it unofficial like this."

"Yes, miss; thank you, miss."

"My pleasure. Come on then, over my lap."

Nicky adopted the position, trying not to think who was doing this to her.

Slapp!

Slapp!

Slapp! Slapp! Slapp! Slapp! Slapp! Slapp! Slapp!

Claire gave her twenty, methodically counted and with plenty of venom. Nicky had taken worse, but it still hurt. After that, she had to lie on the floor, spread her legs and let Pedro have her. Claire watched, commentated, made suggestions and thoroughly enjoyed herself. So, quite evidently, did Pedro and he was practised at getting a result. Nicky orgasmed helplessly.

"Not bad, not bad," Claire said with glee. "Well, that reception should be starting soon. You look a bit lot and sweaty, Nicky, and a bit come-splattered between the legs. You can use my shower quickly. Pedro, would you like to help her?"

So there was the final humiliation of being washed by Pedro as Claire chatted happily away before Nicky was finally able to dress - Claire put her lock back on - and make a grateful escape.

The reception had barely started when Nicky arrived. Vic was not there yet, nor Claire of course. Trying to forget her recent ordeal, Nicky chatted to other karate people there, discussing techniques and the day's event. She had to 'sir' and 'miss' everyone, of course, because they were free and she was not, but they respected her evident knowledge and she was treated well. Vic arrived and Nicky had just gone over to talk to him when John Sutton arrived and called the six girls over to him.

"I thought you all did very well," he complimented them. "Did you enjoy your day?" The chorus of 'yes, master' replies was almost in unison. "Still, you've been allowed to mix on equal terms with free people for long enough, I feel. Do you all have your locks on?" The 'yes, master' chorus this time was rather less enthusiastic. "Then I think you should be dressed appropriately. And then enjoy your evening!"

The six girls quietly removed their clothes. Everything was put into a bin liner which Debbie, the team captain, passed on to Ian to be put away somewhere. A now naked Nicky went back to Vic, sitting on a settee opposite him. He studiously looked at the ceiling: he had always been a complete gentleman with her.

"You may as well have a good look, Vic; everybody else does," she said resignedly.

"That doesn't make it right," Vic replied, still staring at the ceiling.

"Right and wrong are peculiar concepts around this city. Come on: you'll see me nude in the arena next Saturday, so let's get it over with now instead of putting me off my stride then."

Uncertainly, Vic lowered his eyes and looked at her. Nicky felt herself go red, but made her keep her arms away from her private parts. She felt her own hot cheek. "You know, you've made me blush," she said lightly. "It's not often I do that anymore."

"You're very beautiful," he said slightly huskily; "but then, I always knew that."

"Why, thank you, kind sir."

"Nicky, how are we going to get you out of this place?"

Nicky sighed. "You can't. They won't let me leave and there's no way to smuggle me out."

"I can make a huge fuss when I get back, create an international outcry."

She shook her head. "They'll make us all swear that we are here voluntarily. Trust me, they can do that, even for the bravest and toughest. Or they'll remove all evidence of us before they let outside agencies in, and call you a liar. Either way it'll be bad for all the girls."

"I can't just leave you here."

"I honestly wouldn't leave before the end of the season even if I could. After that ... I couldn't go back now. What I've been through has changed me too much. Don't ask. Just ... you never saw me."

"Is that really what you want?"

"It's not about what I want. I don't think I could face the outside world again. And like I said, there's no way of doing it anyhow. Please let's change the subject. I'm going to ask my owner about extending your visas until next weekend: he's got plenty of influence. And maybe he'll let you stay with us at his mansion."

"What about Claire?"

Nicky grimaced, but she was not going to say what had happened upstairs. "She'll be fine here," she assured him truthfully, thinking about Pedro. "Trust me on that one."

On the way to see Mr. Sutton, she met Claire. The blonde looked her up and down and said, "just can't keep your clothes on, can you Nicky?"

"No, miss."

"I left Pedro back in the wardrobe to recharge. Perhaps I should have brought him down with me. But then, he wouldn't be on the guest list."

Nicky thought briefly about the muscular young Spaniard stood in the darkness of the closet. For a moment she wondered if Pedro would 'recharge' by thinking about what he had recently done to her, or his coming liaison with Claire. It was something of an antidote to the few minutes that Claire spent discussing Nicky's 'cellulite, thickening waist, sagging boobs' and so on. Eventually she was able to get away and reach the side of her owner.

"Hello Nicky," he said genially, and gave her the up and down glance he usually did. His eyes narrowed slightly. "Have you been spanked?"

Her bum was still red. "Yes, master." The evidence was obvious. Everybody else in the room could probably spot it if they looked - and most of the men, at least, usually did.

"A bit of horse play with that stud your friend persuaded me to let you go with?"

"She's not my ..." Nicky hesitated; it was not wise for her to contradict something said by a free woman. Instead: "master, perhaps you could ask my old karate coach about my relationship with her. And speaking of him ..."

CHAPTER TEN
Vic

It was like a dream, tinged with the stuff of nightmares.

To find Nicky alive was so wonderful; to find her enslaved, forced to do unspeakable things, was awful. And yet the girl was surviving; no, more than that, she was thriving.

The man she called (almost proudly) her owner did indeed sort out my visa extension and invited me to stay at his mansion, where Nicky and the other five girls lived along with several other slaves and servants of both sexes who waited on me hand and foot.

I watched Nicky in training on Monday. She always loved working hard and she was certainly put through her paces. The girls seemed to quite happily accept their trainer, Ian, pushing them until they almost dropped and putting a strap across their bottoms if he felt they could have put in the slightest extra effort. I know they had no choice but it was more than that: they absolutely did not mind. But then, I had always known that in the old days Nicky would have taken that from me. She was that sort of a girl.

It had been agreed that their karate club would run each night from Monday to Thursday that week with me coaching it. I was shown to a changing room and was getting into my kit when the six girls came in and also got changed. Apparently changing rooms here were communal. They stripped naked in front of me without hesitation, even Nicky, who had never been like that in the old days. But then, they had gone naked at the reception and I wasn't seeing anything I hadn't already seen then. They were laughing and joking and giggling, but on the session that vanished and they were dedicated, attentive and disciplined. Nicky had trained them well.

The showers afterwards were also communal and the girls were back in giggle mode. Two of them were determined to help me shower. Well, I'm no prude. Still, it was rather difficult to keep control.

I was lying in bed later on, reflecting on the day, when there was a knock on my door. One of the girls came in. She was stark naked.

"Hello, uh, Sadie, isn't it?"

"Yes, sir. May I join you?"

I politely said yes, but I hadn't expected her to get into the bed with me and snuggle up. Within a minute or two, it was plain that she was offering her body to me. Aware that she was a coerced slave, I naturally, gently declined.

At breakfast the next morning, Nicky took me on one side. "You turned Sadie down last night," she opened.

I raised my eyebrows. "Word travels fast around here."

"If you didn't fancy her, if there was another girl you'd rather have, it can easily be arranged."

"Don't be silly: she's a lovely girl. But she's, what, nineteen, twenty? I'm fifty-one. She didn't come to me because she wanted to, she came because she was ordered. I'm not going to take advantage of the poor kid like that. It would be tantamount to rape."

Nicky brushed this aside. "She's had a lot worse; we all have. I've told her what a kind, wonderful man you are, dedicated to helping others, honourable, upright, brave. She's quite happy to serve."

"Thank you for the compliment; but it's still not right."

"Do you remember when you took me to Japan on that training trip? You told me that it was important to observe local customs: it was their land, so we should do things their way. 'When in Rome', you said."

I pondered this, then looked Nicky directly in the eye. She had never lied to me. "Are you telling me that she will be quite happy with this?"

"Yes. And so would any other girl here. It's just that she's the one not on the squad at the moment, so she's the one free for such things."

She left it at that. Sadie came to me again that night. We talked for a long time, and eventually, yes, I did it with her. She seemed perfectly happy. I only hope she was.

Tuesday, Wednesday, Thursday went by. The time spent with Nicky was wonderful, although she never neglected her training for a minute. Sadie came to me every night. On Friday there was only very light training, to rest the girls ready for the match. Nicky was noticeably more tense and nervous than I had seen her. I had hardly ever seen her this worked up before a karate championship.

"Matches are ordeals, Vic," she confided to me. "Tomorrow will hurt."

"Are you still sure you want me there?"

"Yes. I want you to be proud of me."

"I'll always be proud of you."

She kissed me - something else she never used to do - and changed the subject.

The arena was filling up. This was Nicky's team's home venue, Slag Stadium. She told me it seated four hundred and it looked like every seat was taken, the vast majority being men.

Claire arrived. I hadn't seen much of her during the week and the muscular young Spaniard on her arm was a good indication why. Well, she was old enough to look after herself. Nicky seemed to know about the young man, although she wouldn't be drawn.

The centre of the arena looked horrific, like a middle ages torture chamber. There were stocks, whipping posts and all sorts of things whose purpose I couldn't - and didn't want to - guess at.

The two teams, each of three girls, marched in to stirring rock music and wild applause. Nicky looked tense and pale. She looked over to me once and managed a weak smile, then did not look my way again.

One by one, the girls stepped up onto a platform and stripped themselves naked. Nicky stepped up in her turn and revealed herself like the rest. I noticed she got huge applause: she was very popular with the crowd. I also noticed her face go red.

The events started. The run, naked, around the athletic track on the edge of the arena stage was first. Nicky's team took first, second and fourth places, with Nicky second to that slim little girl Katie. Then came the orgasm event. To have to have something like that up you in public! And to have to gyrate and bring yourself off.

I found out at last what the nipple rings were for. The pain it must cause, with heavy weights hanging down from her tits like that! There were tears in Nicky's eyes, but she endured and her team won. Then the other rings, which I'd assumed were for the padlocks, were shown to have another more important use. I shuddered in sympathy as Nicky laboured bow-legged down the track, carrying heavy logs by her labia. But she pushed herself hard even so. Her team were winning and she was at the forefront of her team's efforts. I cringed as she was whipped and tormented and humiliated, but she stuck it out and her friends did the same. The final score was 6-3 to Sutton's Slags.

I watched, still stunned from what I had seen, as one of the opposition girls was publicly shaven and then the three girls went into the stocks. Sixty cane strokes each! It was barbaric. I was horrified to note that Claire was watching avidly with a gleam in her eye. How could she be this cruel? Then, as the losing team and their two other girls, also stripped now, were tied down on mattresses, their legs forced apart and long queues forming for each, I watched Nicky and her two friends were taken up to the stocks. Fifteen times the cane buried itself into Nicky's shapely young rear. She yelled in pain but still managed to take it with dignity. When she was released from the stocks, she came down to where I was sitting in the guest seats in the front row. Sweat was pouring from her body, there were bruises and marks all over her and fifteen angry red marks stood out on her bare bottom.

"Nicky," was all I could say, but I think the word carried more sympathy than any long speech could have.

She shrugged and forced a smile, although she must have been in considerable pain. "It's not so bad and it's over now. They're a very good side: they were fourth in the table this morning. It keeps us right on the Tits' tail and keeps our event difference better. We've only got to beat the Tits when they come here and we've won the league." A little glint came into her eye. "In the meantime, which of these five girls are you going to have? The oriental is supposed to be quite good and her queue's not too long."

I looked at the five girls suffering under a series of rapists. "Forget it," I said firmly.

I didn't see much of Nicky for the rest of the day and evening; I gather she had duties, which was fair enough. I went to bed, still troubled by the barbarism I had seen and the suffering of my poor former pupil.

There was a knock on my door at the usual time. "Come in, Sadie," I said, preoccupied.

It wasn't Sadie: it was Nicky. She was stark naked, carrying a piece of paper which she put to one side. The bruises on her body had come out, great big black spots. The weals on her bottom had turned purple and she moved slightly gingerly.

I couldn't think of anything to say. She sat - very carefully - on the foot of the bed and after a strained silence she said coquettishly, "aren't you going to invite me in?"

A wave of affection for her came over me. Moments later she was under the bedclothes with me, snuggling up close to me. She winced as I hugged her, accidentally pressing against the bruises, but hugged me back even tighter.

After a while, I asked, "how long before you recover from all this?"

She shrugged. "Monday or Tuesday, usually. A few of the marks are still visible by Wednesday."

"It was horrible."

She smiled thinly. "I did tell you it's always quite an ordeal."

"You were phenomenally brave, even for you."

She wriggled with pleasure. "Let's see how I am when the Tits come to visit. That's the crunch match."

"How many more matches until the end of the season?"

"Eight, counting that one. Not too long to go."

"And then?"

"I get a nice long holiday, with only a few restrictions and duties."

"And you still don't want me to find a way out of all this for you."

"There's no way out and I'm too far gone anyway. Let's not talk about that."

"All right. Oh, if you can stay, we'd better put Sadie off coming."

"I already have, and I can stay all night."

I will admit to the slightest pang of disappointment: I'd come to enjoy my trysts with the lovely Sadie. But this was my last night here, the last hours I would spend with this wonderful and beautiful girl of whom I was so fond and that was much more important. Then I noticed that Nicky was looking at me slightly strangely. "What?" I asked.

"Are you regretting that you won't get one last chance to get your end away?"

"Of course not. I'd much rather be with you." It was true.

"Well, you won't miss out." She reached for the piece of paper. "Read this."

It was on John Sutton's personal notepaper, dated today. "Dear Vic," it went, "Nicky has my permission for any and all sexual activities tonight. Enjoy with my compliments, John Sutton."

"I went and asked," she said soberly. "I want the honour of serving you fully."

"Nicky," I began, holding her sensual and gorgeous body tight to me, "I couldn't ..."

"Don't make me beg you, Vic," she said softly.

It was a wonderful, tender and yet erotic night, the sort you remember forever. In the morning, all six girls lined up naked, three of them currently rather bruised and marked, to hug and kiss me and say goodbye. As they took my luggage out, I shook hands with John Sutton.

"Please," I implored him, "look after Nicky."

He smiled. "She's a very good asset. I look after all my assets."

"But what will become of her in the end?"

"Most girls can only take a couple of years in the arena. After that, they get sold to private owners. But I make sure all my girls get good owners who will look after them."

It was as good as I could hope for, I suppose. I shook hands with him again and went outside.

Claire was waiting for me. She was in a rickshaw-type cart pulled by two naked, sweating girls harnessed to it. Each had a wooden bit in her mouth just like a horse and their panting breath was whistling past the bit. She held reins and a long, snaking carriage whip in her hands and I saw suspicious red lines on the bare backs of the two girls.

I had become aware this week just how cruel Claire was. I noticed that John Sutton, after asking me about their relationship at the reception, had kept Nicky away from her and I surmised that was for Nicky's protection. It brought home to me how vulnerable and defenceless Nicky's status here left her and I was in some anguish about leaving her to her fate, but she had been right: I had made some discreet enquiries and there was no way they would let her go, or that I could get her away without their permission. And it had been made clear to me that any publicity that I caused back home would have "unfortunate repercussions" for her. I just had to leave her.

A second cart was waiting for me. I climbed into the seat and my eyes were filled by the sight of two young and bare female bottoms. I noted some fresh and some fading red marks. Well, they would pull me to the airport, but I would not lash them.

Claire cracked the whip over the backs of her two pony girls and her cart started off. I cracked the air with mine and my two girls began to pull me away.

EPILOGUE

Nicky stood, dizzy with exhaustion and pain. Every inch of her body was in unbelievable agony. And yet, her heart was soaring as she stared up at the scoreboard.

Sutton's Slags 6, Tibbet's Tits 3.

Five naked girls, three of them covered in weals and welts, were lined up by the stirrups chair. In view of what was riding on this match, the league organisers and the two owners had decreed that the whole squad of the losers would be shaved. Neither team of girls had any say in the matter, but neither would have protested anyway: winning this meant too much to them.

Nicky could hear nothing but the roar of the home crowd in her ears. The celebrations seemed to be shaking the very building to its foundations. There wasn't even the usual hush before the losing team took the first strokes of their caning: in fact, the yells of pain of the Tits could not be heard above the tumult. The two other girls in the Tits squad were already being shagged mercilessly on the rape racks. Just about every single man in the four hundred crowd was lining up in one of the five queues. It wouldn't beat the record set when Nicky and her team had lost at the Theatre Of Anguish and been had by nearly six hundred (with Katie also taking her share) and in a strange way she was pleased by that.

The other Slag girls came over to join her. She and the two others who had competed hugged each other fiercely, not caring about their wounds. Katie, who had not been picked for the final match and Hannah, the other unused squad member and Sadie, had all been on the edge throughout the match, living every moment and supporting to their utmost. Now all three had stripped themselves naked to be fully with their comrades and there were hugs all round. As Nicky and many others later said to the media, it had been a team effort throughout the season, amassing the event difference that finally won the league. It had been incredibly close: never before had one team, let alone two, come right through the season with only one defeat. As they set off on their naked lap of honour, all six of the girls were near orgasm.

The celebrations went on late into the night at Slagland. Champagne flowed freely. Not one of the girls wore a stitch of clothing, or wanted to. At one point, the six girls dived on John Sutton and Ian the trainer and ripped their clothes off. Debbie, the team captain, issued a challenge to the two men to fuck the six girls, three each. The challenge was met firmly. The girls got to choose which one they wanted and Nicky, although Ian was the more dishy, unhesitatingly chose her owner. The men, also in rampant spirits, just about got through the challenge but by the end of it the girls had drained them dry.

A week later, at Slag Stadium, the trophy was formally presented in front of several hundred cheering fans and the TV cameras. The big silver trophy was received by John Sutton on behalf of the team. The girls, all stark naked, held it aloft and went on another lap of honour with it. Then they were to receive their own rather unique trophies. On six chairs, six big dildoes stood proudly up. Each girl went and stood before a chair and lowered herself onto the lubricated dildoes, gasping as they went in. There were straps on the front and backs of the dildoes and these led to a waist band inscribed with 'Corvalle League Champions 2004'. Nicky was soon walking around proudly with her dildo very visibly disappearing inside her and feeling, astonishingly for a slave, on top of the world.

THE END

CPSIA information can be obtained
at www.ICGtesting.com
Printed in the USA
LVHW041946130821
695291LV00005B/671